"Are you certain you want me to leave, Amanda? You practically melted in my arms."

Ty was standing in front of Amanda, facing her, his stance aggressive. His hair was mussed, and his eyes were darkened, still smoldering with the embers of desire. He was by far the sexiest man she'd ever met. Every cell in his body exuded masculinity. He had bedroom eyes, a bedroom voice, and a bedroom physique—along with the soul of a serpent, she reminded herself.

"I've never been more certain of anything in my life," Amanda said. "You used me, Tyler."

"You thought I used you, Mandy. You wanted to believe the worst. Why? At least tell me why?" Ty asked.

"Can you deny it? You made love to me, you made me fall in love with you, and then you convinced me to help you. How could I help but think you used me?"

"We couldn't help falling in love," Ty said. "Or at least I couldn't help it. The one thing I do know is that what we shared was the most meaningful thing in my life."

Jan Mathews

Although she grew up on a farm in a small southern Illinois town and has lived in Chicago for over twenty-five years, Jan Mathews was born in Kentucky and still calls it home. She is a wife, mother, registered nurse, and writer—sometimes in that order. With a son who has a rock band and two other children who are involved in a variety of activities, she is always busy. If she could have one wish in life it would be forty-eight-hour days. She swears that her family, as well as every volunteer organization known to man, senses that she is a soft touch. She has been active in Scouting, athletic clubs, and in the PTA.

Jan's idea of heaven would be to spend a week in the wilderness—minus poison ivy—camping and backpacking. She would love to raft the Chattooga, see the Grand Canyon on horseback, and watch Monday Night Football *without being interrupted.*

Other Second Chance at Love books by
Jan Mathews

A FLAME TOO FIERCE #70
SEASON OF DESIRE #141
NO EASY SURRENDER #185
SLIGHTLY SCANDALOUS #226
THIEF OF HEARTS #273
SHADY LADY #306
NAUGHTY AND NICE #343
HANKY-PANKY #371
EVERYBODY'S HERO #405
STRANGER FROM THE PAST #422
SURRENDER THE DAWN #430

Dear Reader:

With winter drawing its final breath, I invite you to wait out the cold with this month's heartwarming love stories from Second Chance at Love. Veteran authors Steffie Hall and Jan Mathews have come through once again with humor, drama, and, best of all, romance!

As soon as irrepressible veterinarian Jake Elliott sees Amy Klasse, he's hooked. Undaunted when she loses half her skirt to a tricky car door, Amy marches into the local grocery store, wreaking havoc down every isle she strolls—unknowingly observed by a smitten admirer. Unemployed, but always adventurous, Amy finds herself accepting dinner and a job from this handsome hero. Though Jake is more than happy to have come to the rescue, he finds that helping Amy isn't always that easy. Accused of murdering the very rooster that has stolen her spot on a local kiddie television show, Jake has to prove that Amy is incapable of foul play. As Amy and Jake search for clues to prove her innocence, they uncover a mutual passion for each other, and a wonderful and unexpected mystery that demands to be solved. *Foul Play* (#456) by Steffie Hall is a delightful romp filled with humor and adventure.

Dr. Amanda Pearson has more than a few objections when Tyler Marshall comes back to town. Two years before, Amanda had provided Tyler with the crucial testimony he needed to win the biggest case the town of Rialto had ever seen. More than that, Amanda had given Tyler her heart. But when the trial was over, Tyler was gone and Amanda vowed never to get mixed up with the likes of him again. But now Ty's back with a new case to try. And he finds the courtroom battlefield nothing compared with the ground he has to make up with Amanda. Though the attraction is apparent more than ever, Amanda can't ignore the powerful memories—good and bad—that emerge. Can Tyler's seductive powers of persuasion get past Amanda's defense? Jan Mathews gives us a "keeper" in *The Rialto Affair* (#457).

Keep an eye out for Berkley's other February releases. Of *Pulse Points* by Suzanne Topper, Sidney Sheldon says: "A glamorous and intriguing tale of suspense. Solid entertainment!" *Pulse Points* is an opulent, intricate, sizzling new novel of deceit and desire . . . Gaia Gerald had worked to become one of Ferrante's finest jewelry designers. And yet, her success was nothing compared to the fortune she so mysteriously inherited . . . Ugo Ferrante, the patriarch of the international jewelry empire, bequeathed his New York store to the lovely Gaia. What deadly secrets led him to leave a fortune to a woman he'd given *nothing* to during his life? Suzanne Topper provides continuous excitement in this first-rate work of fiction. And from Jill Gregory, the two-million-copy bestselling author of *Moonlit Obsession,* comes *Looking Glass Years,* her most captivating novel. A woman who dared to dream, Elly Forrest's life was filled with laughter, joy, and heartache. From the industrial boom of Pittsburgh in the late 1800s to the windswept grandeur of Chicago, she held fast to her visions of success, despite the odds . . . Despite the handsome brute she married, the spoiled aristocrat who ravaged her sister, and the fire that nearly destroyed her passion and the one man she loved more than life itself. And, finally, February brings you a spectacular new novel from the author of *Wild Heart Tamed* and *The Tender Devil. Affaire de Coeur* calls author Colleen Shannon "a sparkling new talent!" and we couldn't agree more. *The Hawk's Lady* brings us Lady Victoria. Beautiful and boldly defiant, she sailed away from England to escape an obligation of marriage. Then the unthinkable happened—her ship was captured by Barbary pirates. Captain Sinan Reis, the pirate known as the "Hawk" would shun vast profit to claim the English beauty for himself. The evil Ahmet, a Turkish rogue, defied Captain Reis by stealing his precious lady. The aging Dey, chief of Algiers, held the power to possess—or destroy—them all. Tory's heart was imprisoned by fate, and yet, her secret passion for her pirate captor bound her soul to his. Together on an odyssey of exotic peril, they would challenge an empire . . .

Excitement, adventure, passion . . .

Until next month—happy reading!

Hillary Cige

Hillary Cige, Editor
SECOND CHANCE AT LOVE
The Berkley Publishing Group
200 Madison Avenue
New York, NY 10016

JAN MATHEWS
THE RIALTO AFFAIR

BERKLEY BOOKS, NEW YORK

THE RIALTO AFFAIR

First edition published February 1989

ISBN: 0-425-11401-5

Second Chance at Love books are published by
The Berkley Publishing Group
200 Madison Avenue, New York, NY 10016

Printed in the United States of America

10 9 8 7 6 5 4 3 2 1

THE RIALTO AFFAIR

Chapter One

DR. AMANDA LOUISE PEARSON had been digging in her flower beds when old Jimmy John Morris came over to ask her to stitch up the cut on his hand. It was Sunday and her office was closed, but as the only doctor in the small hamlet of Rialto, Illinois, Amanda was available twenty-four hours a day. Now, properly cleaned, stitched, and bandaged, Jimmy John was changing the water pump on her beat-up Camaro. He was the town mechanic, and her ancient car was his bone of contention. It was almost with delight that he'd noticed the small pool of antifreeze on her driveway.

Amanda grimaced at the grease that was already accumulating on his hands. "If you get that wound dirty, I swear I'll give you the biggest shot of penicillin you've ever set your eyes on, Jimmy John."

The old man just shook his head. "You need a new car, Doc. This thing ain't gonna last much longer. It's nigh on older 'n me. 'sides, I told you before, a pretty young gal like you should have a sporty, good-lookin' car."

"I'm attached to this one." Amanda could no more afford a new car than visit the moon. The entire town knew she was mortgaged to the hilt.

"Hah!" Jimmy John sccffed. "I was attached to my rabid dog, too, but I had sense enough to get rid of it. Mark my words, Mandy Lou, one of these days you're gonna break down."

Amanda knew he had inadvertently called her by her childhood name. She had discovered that was one of the disadvantages of practicing medicine in her hometown. Quite often the townspeople remembered her as a child.

He pointed to the water pump. "Now try and get that bolt in place while I hold this thing right. I swear I can't understand what's taking you so long. Can't you see the orifices? They're as big as a city pothole."

"I can *see* the orifices," Amanda complained, "I just can't reach them." She swiped a hand across the errant lock of blond hair that had fallen from her French braid and tucked it into place as she bent over the engine. It was hot today and rivulets of sweat ran between her breasts. Although she had washed up before suturing Jimmy John's cut, she still felt grimy. This was lawn-mowing day and she'd determined to plant some flowers around the front entrance to her combination office/home. Early on, she'd changed into cutoff jeans and a bright blue half-shirt that proclaimed her a Chicago Cubs fan. Now her clothes were as dusty and filthy as her body.

"Got it?" the old man asked. "Get the next one now. Say, ain't that something about young Tommy Whittiker?" he went on in his gossipy fashion, his head bent to the task. "I just can't believe that boy would do something so foolish as hurting his friend so bad. Over a girl, too. Some folks figured he'd be trouble when his mamma and daddy shipped him home to Rialto to live with his grandfolks all those years ago, but it sure is hard to reckon he'd do something that terrible."

All but ignoring his prattle, Amanda tried to insert the next bolt. As a physician, she couldn't talk about the Tommy Whittiker case. Although, even if she could answer, Jimmy John didn't expect much of an explanation. No one did, but in the tiny village of twelve hundred, this latest scandal was the hottest topic since the town spinster, Miss Polly, had gotten pregnant and run off with an insurance salesman last year. For the past week, the Tommy Whittiker, Bobby Martin, and Sandy Samuels love triangle had been explored, exploited, embellished, and exaggerated to the extreme.

According to gossip, after discovering his girl friend was pregnant with his best friend's child, Tommy Whittiker had purposely run down Bobby Martin with his motorcycle, smashing the boy against a tree. Both teenagers were in the hospital in Parkersville, but Bobby Martin was in critical condition. It was such a shame; they were only nineteen and the accident would affect them for the rest of their lives.

"You treated Tommy that night they brought them in, didn't you, Doc?" Jimmy John asked. "The hospital called you. Do you think you'll have to testify?"

That was a likely possibility. Amanda had already been questioned by the sheriff. And as much as she liked Tommy Whittiker, the fact was, he'd been drinking that night. The odor of alcohol had been readily apparent on his breath and on his clothing. The authorities were only waiting for the test results.

"You think it was intentional?" The old man kept probing. "You think Tommy meant to hurt Bobby? I know he threatened him and all, but that was just kid stuff. He was madder than a hornet, though. Folks over in Senton, they think Tommy's guilty as sin."

The entire episode was shaded by the fact that the two towns had always been rivals. Bobby Martin was from Senton and Tommy Whittiker was from Rialto, but they'd been close friends since meeting on the football field during their freshman year of high school.

"Wonder who's the big-gun criminal lawyer the Whittikers is hiring? I hear tell he's from Chicago." Jimmy John pronounced it like all the residents of Rialto, as *Sheecago*. "Say, didn't you take your doctoring there?"

"Yes." Although it was a simple question, Amanda had to repress sudden, poignant memories. The pain was as fresh today as it had been two years ago when she'd left Chicago and come back home. "I served my residency at County Memorial."

"I thought so. I remembered it was Sheecago."

If Jimmy John recalled the rest of the story, he didn't mention it. There'd been a scandal then, too, one that had involved her and a famous criminal lawyer. But when Amanda had met Gordon Tyler Marshall, he wasn't well-known. He'd been a struggling young attorney on his way up, eager to right the wrongs of the world. She'd been a studious medical resident, eager to give her love and trust. Unfortunately for her, what Ty Marshall had really craved was renown. It was after he'd used her that he'd become a national celebrity.

She'd been an unwitting pawn in his scheme to attain fame and fortune.

That was one of the reasons she'd come home—to heal. The last she'd heard, Ty had moved from Chicago. He was living in New York and working in a prestigious law firm. He had tried to contact her several times. Once he'd even come to Rialto, but she had refused to see him. Thankfully, over the years, the town's curiosity surrounding the incident had died a natural death, but Amanda had never fully resolved her feelings about him, or about the case. Now, the mere thought of him opened all the old wounds, and the Tommy Whittiker case was so much like the one in Chicago where she'd testified for Ty that she felt an odd sense of déjà vu.

"Got that bolt, Mandy Lou?" Jimmy John asked her. "They's four of them, so try to get the one on the opposite side now. Pump'll be balanced. You know, if the Whittikers is getting a Sheecago lawyer, they're gonna pay plenty. Good thing Tommy's daddy's loaded. 'Course, it ain't like there's anybody here in Rialto that can help 'em. Since old Elmer passed on, the closest lawyer that knows his stuff is in Effingham. Sure is a chore goin' all the way over there to get up a will or a contract."

Amanda nodded, figuring he expected an occasional reaction. "Yes, it is a problem."

"Yup, well, ain't nobody interested in my opinion, but I think Tommy's innocent. Never will forget the day that boy came to town. He roared in here on his motorcycle and expected me to drop everything to fix it. Spoiled brat he was, but he growed-up pretty good. I thought he turned out to be a right nice kid, and I had that motorcycle running just fine."

While the old man jabbered away, Amanda tried to concentrate on the bolts. One more to go. She heard a car pull up to the curb and a car door open and close, but she resisted the impulse to look up from her task. It was probably another patient, and if she didn't get the damned bolts in soon, Jimmy John would try the Whittiker case on her front lawn. And he might find something else wrong with her car.

Jimmy John leaned over to inspect a rusty, round object under the hood. "This here engine is sick, Doc. Look at that distributor. It's a pity. Why don't you let me give the old gal a complete overhaul? If you don't want to bring it into the shop, I can take it apart right here and now."

"The car's fine," Amanda answered. Taking her engine apart was the last thing she needed. With a grunt she draped herself over the fender even farther, twisting the bolt as hard as she could. Although the footsteps coming up the driveway paused, Amanda ignored them, curiosity about her visitor tempered by her concern over the water pump. Whoever it was could just wait. After all, it *was* Sunday, and in Rialto there weren't too many medical emergencies.

"Well, I'll be, a silver Mercedes. Howdy there, stranger." Jimmy John spoke in his friendly manner. "You don't seem too sick, but if you're looking to see the doc, she's right here. We got a little car problem. Be finished right soon. This old beater's more trouble than it's worth. I keep telling Mandy Lou to bring it in for an overhaul, but she's as stubborn as a mule."

"I can wait."

The voice was deep, masculine, and heart-wrenchingly familiar. Amanda paused, willing her hands to stop their sudden trembling. It couldn't be Ty—not here, not now. Fate wouldn't be that cruel. Her mind was playing tricks on her. The mention of a criminal lawyer had brought back the memories.

"Besides," the voice went on in a low, intimate tone, "I'm enjoying the view."

Jimmy John glanced around at the blossoming shrubs and stately trees with pride. "Yup, well, Rialto is a mighty purty little town. I kinda like the view, too."

Amanda felt her entire body flush red. The view the man was talking about had nothing to do with the town. She jerked her head up and hit the back of her skull on the edge of the hood. A sharp stab of pain shot through her and she could feel the sensation of blood slowly oozing from a cut. She managed to turn around just as the man stepped in front of the car. She closed her eyes for a moment, hoping the bump on her head was responsible for the vision wavering before her eyes.

But the injury wasn't clouding her reasoning. It was Gordon Tyler Marshall in the flesh, standing in front of her, every magnificent inch of him.

It was hard to accept that two years had passed, Amanda thought as her gaze met and held his deep blue one. Aside from a few sprinkles of gray at the temples, Ty Marshall looked the same as the last time she'd seen him. Tall and lean and ruggedly handsome, his austere three-piece suit stretched perfectly over his broad shoulders—shoulders that were too wide for a lawyer. She'd always thought he had the physique of a construction worker, and his tanned skin and thick dark hair only added to that image.

"Hello, Amanda," he said with the same irresistible smile that had always driven her wild. For one breathless moment she felt the earth spin. Her knees went weak and her heart started to do flip-flops. Her throat was dry and her breath came in rapid gasps. Jimmy John saved her from having to speak.

"Hey!" the old man suddenly proclaimed. "Ain't you that Marshall feller, the famous criminal lawyer?" Grinning broadly, he held out his hand. "Well, I'll be dadblamed. I watched you on television just the other night. You got that lady in Houston an acquittal. I'm Jimmy John Morris."

Tyler smiled and extended his hand. "Just call me Ty. And for the record, the lady in Houston happened to be innocent."

"Well, you sure was something. They say you razzle-dazzled the jury, just like every other time. You here to defend Tommy Whittiker?"

"Among other things." As always, the husky, intimate quality of Ty's voice shivered along Amanda's spine. Each time he spoke, he sounded like he'd either just gotten out of bed or was headed for one. "I have a little personal business here, too."

"Personal business?" Jimmy John echoed.

Ty nodded, glancing at Amanda. "Since I'm going to be here for a while, I thought I might take the opportunity to renew an old acquaintance."

Wonderful. Although their affair had been brief, it had been as fiery as a forest fire raging out of control. Amanda closed her eyes again to dispel the memories, to blot out the sudden urge to touch him, to feel his strong arms around her. When she opened them, Ty was studying her intently, his gaze lingering along the curve of her breasts, the slight swell of her hips. The intimate glance, so fraught with knowledge of her body, brought back a rush of emotion that spread through her like wildfire. She reached for a rag to wipe her hands, hoping the forced movement would exorcise the memory of what it felt like to have his hands caress her, to have his lips possess hers.

"What do you want, Ty?" The question came out sharp, angry. By now she could feel the sticky blood crusting her hair. Scalp wounds were very vascular and even tiny ones bled a lot, but she ignored it. Her clotting mechanism was normal, evidently neither man had noticed, and there were too many conflicting emotions churning inside her right now to worry about a minor cut.

"We could start with a cool glass of lemonade," Ty answered. "It's hot here."

He didn't want lemonade any more than she wanted to take apart her car. Tyler drank scotch. He just didn't want to talk in front of Jimmy John. Neither did she, but she didn't want to talk at all. In fact, she didn't even want to *see* Tyler Marshall.

"There's a café on Main Street that serves the very best lemonade in town." Turning away, she slammed down the hood of her car. "Try there. I'm a doctor, not a restaurant."

Jimmy John looked from one of them to the other. This time the old man didn't miss the tension, nor did he misinterpret Amanda's sudden animosity. "Well, I'll be dad-blamed. You two know each other? Why, 'course you do." He answered his own question. "I'll be dog-danged."

He shifted back and forth, not from embarrassment,

but from excitement. Amanda could tell that Jimmy John could hardly wait to get to town and spread the news. For the next several days he would be the center of attention—if not because he was the first person in Rialto to remember that Dr. Amanda Louise Pearson was acquainted with Gordon Tyler Marshall, then because he was the first to witness their reunion. The previous scandal would be resurrected from the town gossip mortuary to be recounted over and over, elaborated and enhanced until neither Amanda nor Tyler would recognize either story.

"Yes," she answered angrily, "we know each other. In fact, we're old friends."

But Jimmy John wasn't waiting for her confirmation. He had bent down to gather up his tools. "Well, I got to be going. Don't want to hold you up or nothing. Now you bring that car in whenever you can, Doc. Only you better do it soon, 'fore you get stuck out in the middle of nowhere with nothing 'cept your feet to get you back home. See you all later."

Amanda didn't bother to say good-bye. Not wanting to give him any further gossip to impart, she waited until he had scurried off in the direction of town. She felt foolish standing on her driveway with a rag in her hand, and she felt even more foolish when she looked down at herself. Her legs and thighs were dusty all the way down to her torn gym shoes. Thick smudges of grease crisscrossed her cutoff jeans, and her hands were grimy, one nail broken off.

She had sometimes dreamed of confronting Tyler again, but she'd always imagined herself dressed to the hilt in a designer gown, wearing fancy jewels with swept-up hair like the women she'd seen him with in the newspapers and on television. It had been a vengeful fantasy in which she used him and scorned him. Unfortunately, at the moment she didn't even look like a doctor, much less a femme fatale.

"You haven't changed much, Amanda," he said, bringing her back to the present. "You're still as beautiful as ever."

She clutched the rag tightly and stared at him. "You haven't changed much either, Ty. You're still a consummate liar."

"You really believe that, don't you?" He leaned against her car, crossing his arms and placing one foot over the other. His lips twisted into a tight, derisive smile. "Two years ago you convicted me without a trial and you're doing the same thing now. That's a bad habit, Amanda. Justice is usually based on evidence."

"I apologize for disregarding the legal technicalities," she answered, unable to prevent the bitterness that crept into her tone, "but as I recall, you weren't the innocent victim."

"And you were?"

What was the sense of going into it? She didn't want to argue with him. She didn't want to dredge up the memories. "You didn't answer my question, Ty. What is it that you want? I've told you before, I don't want to see you or talk to you."

"Personally, you mean."

"No," she corrected, "I mean in any way."

Amanda had noticed that her closest neighbor, Mrs. Crowley, was pulling nonexistent weeds from around an oak tree by the driveway. Although she lived on a wide, quiet street where the homes were set far back, she knew every eye in the neighborhood was looking out its living room window. Evidently Ty had noticed her neighbor, too. He glanced at Mrs. Crowley, then back to Amanda. "Perhaps we should go inside."

"Right here is fine," she said firmly. She had to end it here and now, on her driveway. She couldn't let Tyler Marshall into her house, back into her life.

"What if I said it's about Tommy Whittiker?"

"Is it?"

"Partly."

Darn the man. Ty knew she couldn't force him to discuss the case outdoors. Ethics were involved and her home was the only place in town that didn't have ears. Mustering as much professional dignity as she could manage considering her state of attire, she gestured to her house. "Then I suppose I must bid you welcome."

"Is it that hard, Amanda?"

"Yes," she said, and turned away.

Amanda's father had bought the sturdy red-brick bungalow she lived in more than fifty years ago. Because he was the town physician, he had planned his offices as part of his home and had gutted the front half. When he'd died, and Amanda had renovated, she'd taken up even more space. The living quarters consisted of two bedrooms, a living room, and an old country kitchen at the back of the house, complete with yellow curtains and matching linoleum.

Amanda led Ty in through the side door. Not bothering with social amenities—if she offered him something to drink, he might misconstrue it as a real welcome—she sat at the kitchen table and indicated the chair across from her. "Now. What about Tommy Whittiker?"

Ty arched an eyebrow at her brusque attitude. "You're not wasting any words."

"Why should I?"

He shrugged. "Old times' sake?"

"Let's get this clear, Ty. As far as I'm concerned, there aren't any old times between us—or there shouldn't have been. That was a mistake I made, and I won't make it again. Now what about Tommy Whittiker? Or was that just another lie?"

He sighed. "No, it wasn't a lie, but I don't expect you'll believe that—you haven't believed anything so far." Then, as though dismissing the subject, he took out a pen and a pad of paper. "Let's start with Tommy's medical records. I'd like to see them."

Amanda smiled. "I'm not too familiar with the procedure, but don't you have to have a court order or something official?" She was being difficult, but her records were private. "If so, I'd like to see it."

"Of course." Unsnapping his briefcase, Tyler pulled out a piece of paper and handed it to her. "I believe you'll find everything in order."

Amanda took the page from him and read it carefully. Without further comment, she went into her office for the file. Ty waited in the kitchen. When she came back she noticed that he had taken off his suit jacket and draped it over a chair. Trying to ignore the fact that he had watched her every move, she handed him the thin manila folder. "Here you are."

"Thank you."

"You're welcome," she answered sweetly.

While Ty studied the contents of the folder, Amanda studied her hands. She needed to wash them. Grease had accumulated under her nails and along her cuticles. Her head was beginning to throb.

He looked up from the folder. "A twisted ankle three years ago, a high school physical with a tetanus booster, and one incident of strep throat. There isn't too much here."

Amanda shrugged. "Tommy's a healthy teenager. What did you expect to find? I can't always provide you with the medical evidence to win your cases."

Once again he flashed that tight, derisive smile that told her he thought she was being unfair. "You're very persistent, Amanda."

"So are you."

"According to my research he has two prior arrests for drunkenness and one charge of public obscenity. Wasn't he injured then? I thought maybe he was in a fight."

They were back to Tommy. "No. On both occasions he had a few beers at the annual town festival and slept it off at home. Last year he accidently ran his motorcycle into Mary Cahill's pigpen. He swore at it in front of Miss Mary. No complaint of injury."

"You didn't examine him?"

"He wasn't hurt." But Amanda was. She reached up to touch her cut and her hand came away with streaks of sticky blood. She started for the sink to wash it. Suddenly, Ty was beside her.

"You're bleeding, Amanda. Here, let me take a look."

Before she could object, he was sifting his fingers through her hair, searching for the cut. He should have been a physician, she thought, his hands were strong yet gently probing, tender yet sure.

"That's a nasty cut. How did it happen?"

"On the hood of my car."

"When I came? I'm sorry."

"It was my own fault."

A lot of things had been her own fault—right from the beginning when she had fallen in love with him. But he didn't confirm or deny her statement. "Where are your supplies?" he asked. "I've had some first-aid training. I'll clean it for you. I think you might need a couple stitches, though."

He sat her at the kitchen table and disappeared into her office. Within moments he was back with a small washbasin, soap, and antiseptic. Quickly and efficiently he cleaned the cut, first unraveling her long braid.

"The blood has dried in your hair," he said softly. "I could brush it for you."

She shook her head. "I can manage later. I'll wash it."

"All right. I still need to clean the wound."

"Fine."

"I'll try not to hurt you."

If only he'd tried not to hurt her before. If only she hadn't fallen in love with him. "Thank you."

"Hold still, now. It'll take me a few minutes."

Amanda wasn't certain how much time passed while he treated her injury. They didn't speak except for minor exchanges, a word here and there, and everything seemed to be happening in slow motion. She sat very still, wincing occasionally as the antiseptic stung her open cut. She felt dazed, dull-witted as she looked around her cheery kitchen. Perhaps she was suffering from a mild concussion.

Something odd was happening to her. Ty had made

himself at home—and she hadn't made a single protest. His suit jacket was still draped over a chair and the sleeves of his snowy-white shirt were rolled up to his elbows. He'd found a comb and was now brushing her hair, his fingers stroking through the strands. He would lift the silky locks and let them fall to fan along her neck. Whenever his touch whispered against her skin she felt prickles of excitement, of the old magnetism between them. She couldn't see his fingers, but she remembered they were long and tapered, the nails blunt and clean. She'd always been fascinated by the corded muscles in his forearms, by the veins that laced his hands like sinewy filaments.

Suddenly, the memory of his caresses, of those hands on her body, surged full force to taunt her. Her skin shivered with remembered desire. She didn't know when he put the comb down and began to gently massage the knots in her shoulders. She sat immobile, spellbound by his touch. He'd always had a hypnotic effect on her, his mere presence creating a lethargy more potent than an opiate. A narcotic on her nerves.

"Mandy..." The seductive timbre of his voice thrilled through her. Still massaging, his fingers stroked the front of her shoulders, moving along her throat, down her sternum. She didn't move; she could hardly breathe as he stroked his thumbs back and forth across her skin. His lips nuzzled the smooth, white column of her neck and his breath whispered in her ear.

A whispered moan escaped from Amanda's throat. Her blood roared and pounded in her head, but before she could succumb to the overwhelming sensations, some protective mechanism finally penetrated her brain. Why was she allowing him to touch her? To kiss her?

Caress her? Two years ago he had used her. He had destroyed her. Panic welled in her mind and a cold, hard determination settled in the pit of her stomach.

"Don't!" she said. Though she felt she could hardly move, she managed to jerk away. "Don't touch me. You're not welcome here, Ty. Please leave." She felt shaky inside and it wasn't all from passion.

"Amanda, listen to me." He started toward her, his hands held out in earnest.

But she was adamant. "No. Don't come near me." Her emotions were a turbulent jumble. Backing away, she clutched at the kitchen counter for strength. Though husky with desire, her words were firm. "I said leave now, Ty. And please don't come here again. I don't want to see you anymore."

He looked as confused as she felt. "Are you crossing your fingers, Amanda? You're not a little girl anymore."

Once she had confessed to him that when she was a little girl she had crossed her fingers whenever she told a fib, hoping she wouldn't be discovered. She held up her hands and looked him squarely in the eye. "No crossed fingers. Go away, Ty, and leave me alone."

"You're lying, Amanda," he said softly.

Yes, she desired him, that she couldn't deny—not even to herself. But she had changed. Bitter experience had been her teacher. "I don't have to defend myself, Ty, especially to you. You're welcome to think whatever you want. I don't care. Just leave before I call the sheriff to put you out."

Ty looked at her for a long time, as though contemplating her words. That was one of his habits. His slow, methodical assessments were disturbing, because a person never quite knew just what he was thinking. "Are you sure, Amanda? Are you certain you want me to leave? You practically melted in my arms."

The arrogant statement made her blood boil, but she tilted her head back in firm resolution, meeting his gaze. He was standing in front of her, facing her, his stance aggressive, all authoritative male. His hair was mussed, falling over his forehead in an appealing slash, and his eyes were darkened, still smoldering with the embers of desire. He was the sexiest, most exciting man she'd ever met. Every cell in his body exuded masculinity. He had bedroom eyes, a bedroom voice, and a bedroom physique—along with the soul of a serpent, she reminded herself.

"I've never been more certain of anything in my life," she said. "You used me, Tyler."

"You thought I used you, Mandy. You wanted to believe the worst. Why? At least tell me why."

"Can you deny it? You made love to me, you made me fall in love with you, and then you convinced me to help you. How could I help but think you used me? I had ample evidence."

"Your testimony gave an innocent man his freedom," he said.

Was that supposed to make her feel righteous? Vindicated? To this day she wasn't certain if her interpretation of the facts two years ago was because of what she had felt for Tyler or what she had felt was the truth. She had spent nights struggling with her conscience, going over and over the details of the trial, wondering if she had seen things his way because she loved him, wondering if his client had really suffered from a disease. Because of the circumstances of the case, she had never reached a conclusion. The emotional battle had torn her apart.

"You never answer a question directly, do you, Ty? Is that something you learned in law school?"

"Maybe I did use you, Mandy," he said. "Maybe I did at first. I'm not sure anymore. Winning that case meant a great deal to me. I would have done anything within the realm of the law to clear Jack Cameron."

"Which is exactly my point."

"I said within the realm of the law, Amanda," he reminded her. "Despite what you may think, I do have morals. You seem to forget that you volunteered to come forward."

"After I fell in love with you."

"Does it matter when?"

"You know it does."

"All right," he agreed again. "Maybe it does matter, but we couldn't help falling in love. Or at least I couldn't help it. The one thing I do know is that what we shared was the most meaningful thing in my life."

Her smile was sardonic. "How convenient to fall in love with the one person who could offer you the evidence to win your case. Why are you here now?"

"Amanda, the only reason I took this case was because you were here. I wanted to see you."

"For what? More suspect medical facts? Conclusions rather than diagnoses? What is it that you need this time, Ty? I was a great expert witness. Is it another case of genetic porphyria? Does somebody else have a metabolic defect that might affect their reasoning? And I say 'might' loosely."

He sighed again. "Amanda, why can't you accept the fact that what you did wasn't unusual?"

"Why can't you accept the fact that what I did was wrong, Ty? I testified—"

"Wrong in whose eyes?" he cut in angrily. "Did you lie? Tell me, did you get up on the witness stand and lie?"

"Of course not," she answered, "but that isn't the point."

"Things that come out on a witness stand can be shaded. I've told you that hundreds of times. You made a conclusion based on test results."

"It was a conclusion other doctors might not have made. You knew that, and you led me to it."

"All I gave you was the test results, Amanda. What you did was all right. What you did was *right*."

"I don't buy it," she answered. "I didn't buy it then, when I found out what you had done, and I don't buy it now." Emotionally she'd felt so used. "I was your last resort, Ty. You tried to get other doctors to testify and you couldn't. Nobody would come forward, nobody credible, that is. Then you found me. How do you think I felt when I discovered that you had known all along about Jack Cameron's background, and that you had presented his illness to me so I would see it your way?"

"At first there were things I couldn't tell you because of secrecy to my client. Then, when you came forward, there were things I couldn't tell you because they *would* have shaded your testimony. Amanda, I wanted you to make your own conclusions."

"Don't you mean you wanted to lead me to my conclusions?"

"Drama is allowed in a courtroom, too."

"It's a good thing. You'd be in big trouble if it wasn't."

He shook his head. "I'm not making excuses. I was committed to my client and to his defense. If I hadn't done everything in my power to clear him, I would have been derelict in my duty. Don't you see, it's my job to find things and present them in a certain light. That's the way things are done in my profession and there's nothing wrong with it."

"Don't *you* see, Ty, you haven't answered my question. I'll ask it again. Did you try to make me know things so I would *see* them your way?"

He stared at her a long moment. "Jack Cameron was innocent."

"And Ty Marshall?" she asked softly. "Was he innocent?"

From his expression, he knew exactly what she was talking about, and more than ever Amanda was convinced that he had pursued her for one reason and one reason alone—to get her to testify.

"How does it feel to be successful, Ty? How does it feel to have everything you've always dreamed of having?"

He paused. "What happened to the appointment you were going to get to the County Memorial staff?"

Just before the scandal had hit, Amanda had been offered a prestigious spot on the staff of the medical center. "They decided to hire someone else."

"Because of the publicity surrounding the trial?"

Amanda shrugged. "They didn't say why." But Amanda knew it was because she had testified for Ty while she was in love with him. The people in her profession considered what she had done an unethical act. Unfortunately, in retrospect, she couldn't disagree. If only she'd realized it before she'd gotten up on that witness stand. If only she'd been *sure* before she'd gotten up on that witness stand.

"I'm sorry."

"Are you?" She glanced at him.

"You know, Amanda, success isn't always what you think it's going to be."

Was that an apology? Did he feel even a bit guilty over what had happened two years ago?

"I wanted to see you," he went on.

"I don't believe you, Ty," she said, deciding he didn't feel guilty at all. How could he? She had already discovered he didn't have any principles. Tyler Marshall was a mendacious bastard, as conscienceless and unprincipled as the devil the preacher raved about on Sunday mornings. "I'm not a naive medical resident anymore. You can't fool me. You came here for one reason and one reason only—to make more of a name for yourself. How are you going to do it this time? What kind of courtroom spectacle are you going to orchestrate?"

"Think about it, Amanda. This isn't the kind of case that does much for a law career."

"Really? Tell me it won't make the news. Tell me the wire services will ignore it, particularly considering the sexual overtones—a young boy involved in a love triangle, a pregnant girl, a critically ill friend. Sex, scandal, notoriety. You thrive on those things, Ty, and don't bother to deny it."

Why did the harsh words come so easily? For a moment time rolled back and he looked as hurt as he had that day in Chicago when he'd begged her to understand, to wait for an explanation. Too wrapped up in her own pain, she hadn't wanted to acknowledge his.

"Can you at least try to see my side of it?" he asked now.

"No," she answered sadly. "No, I can't. As far as I'm concerned you have no defense. You're the worst kind of opportunist, Ty, because you're a predator. You deceive people consciously. Now please leave and don't come back. I've already told you, you're not welcome here. I don't want to see you, speak to you, or hear about you."

"That final?"

"That final," she reiterated.

"You could be wrong."

"I'm not."

His expression fell. "All right, Amanda, if that's the way you want it. I won't fight you anymore. I had to try."

Something drove her to keep hurting him, some demon called vengeance. "Too bad."

Only she'd gone too far. Suddenly a mask seemed to drop over his expression and he began to unroll and button his shirt sleeves, all cold efficiency. "Yes, too bad. I will be in town, though, for the next few weeks, and I doubt if under the circumstances we can avoid all contact. I assume we can still have a professional relationship."

"That's fine with me. As long as we're talking strictly professional."

"Then we're in agreement." Turning from her, he grabbed his suit jacket and shrugged his arms inside. "If it's convenient for you, *Dr. Pearson*, I'd like to go over Tommy Whittiker's hospital chart as soon as I have it copied. And I understand you're waiting for the results of a blood-alcohol level. I presume you'll be kind enough to let me know when it arrives."

"I'll notify you immediately," she responded to his

oddly hurtful use of her title. To her annoyance, she realized her hands were trembling. She didn't want him to leave. She wanted him to drag her off to the bed and make mad, passionate love to her. She *wanted* him to love her forever.

"I don't suppose you tested Tommy for drugs?" he went on.

Amanda shrugged. "There wasn't any indication it was necessary to draw a drug screen. Tommy doesn't have a history of drug abuse and he was obviously drunk."

"Excuse me?" Ty said, whirling around and speaking so swiftly and so angrily that it made her dizzy. "What did you say?"

"Tommy was obviously drunk."

He stepped close to her, his fury evident in his every feature. "Don't ever make that kind of presumption in one of my cases, Amanda. I may have come here because of you, but I'm going to defend that boy to the best of my ability, and Tommy Whittiker is *innocent* until *proven* guilty. It may surprise you, but that happens to be the legal system in this country. *It's called due process of law.*"

"I'm sorry, Ty," she said, immediately regretting her rash assumption. "I didn't mean to imply that Tommy was guilty."

Just as quickly the anger was gone and Ty sighed wearily. He ran a hand through his hair. "I'm sorry, too, Amanda. I shouldn't have snapped at you. It's just that justice means a great deal to me."

"Yes, I remember." He'd told her that once before, a long time ago. She'd believed him then.

"You know, Mandy," he went on after a moment, "you weren't the only one who was hurt."

"You left for New York, Ty. You chose your career."

"You wouldn't see me. What was I supposed to do? Chase you across the city so that you could turn me away? I had three days to make that decision. I'd worked all my life toward a goal, and you said some harsh things."

"Some deserved things," she corrected. "Ty, the subject is exhausted and so am I. Please leave."

"There's nothing I can do to convince you my convictions are honorable?"

She shook her head, steeling herself against the hurt in his tone. "I can't trust you, Ty. I don't think I can ever trust you again. You betrayed me."

Tyler stared at her for a long time, then headed for the door. Just before leaving, he paused. "There's a funny thing about betrayal, Amanda. Guilt or innocence depends on your point of view. If you do change your mind and care to see my side of it, I'll be in town."

Chapter Two

THE DOOR CLOSED SOFTLY and Ty was gone. Amanda sat in thoughtful silence. For a moment, the memories of the past were so vivid she felt as if she were reliving that night two years ago when she had first met him. It had been very late on a Monday night.

Since it was the county hospital, the census was always full. Tests were conducted twenty-four hours a day; surgery was as common at midnight as it was at seven in the morning and the emergency room looked more like a battle zone than an area in a healing facility. She had just been paged to visit the Medical Records Department and sign a few charts. The call had surprised her. Usually she was careful not to forget those things.

Her heels clicked on the cement floor. County Memorial wasn't very fancy. Carpeting was found only in the administrative offices. The bare walls, though clean, were painted gray. Medical Records was squeezed between the morgue and Central Supply. It was a large room stacked with discharged patients' charts.

She smiled at the receptionist as she entered the room. "Hi, Molly, sorry I forgot to sign those charts."

The woman waved away her apology. "I didn't call you here to sign charts. If all the doctors here were as conscientious as you, I wouldn't have a job."

"Thanks," Amanda answered, wondering who had paged her. Perhaps she'd heard the extension wrong. "Well, I guess I'll check with the operator then and head for home. I have final rounds at seven. If I hurry that leaves me about six hours sleep."

"Oh, I paged you," Molly said, nodding toward a man sitting at a table in the back of the room. "This guy wants to talk with you."

Amanda glanced at the man as he stood and stretched wearily. Though the lighting was dim, she could clearly distinguish his features. He was tall and lithe and incredibly sexy. Either he was new to the staff or the nurses were slipping. No one in her right mind would forget to mention him.

Yet he wasn't one of the residents, Amanda thought as he hitched his suit jacket over his shoulder with his thumb and headed toward them. She would have recognized him. He had to be an attending physician, one of the few at Memorial. Only what was an attending doctor doing here this late at night, and in Medical Records? Had she made a mistake in treating one of his discharged patients?

"Thank you." He handed Molly a chart. His voice was like liquid velvet, all smooth and soft and husky.

"My pleasure." Molly flushed, and grinned at him.

To Amanda's knowledge, except for herself, no one had ever thanked the clerk for anything.

Now his attention shifted to Amanda. The attraction was immediate and magnetic. When he smiled she felt her body melt. "You wanted to see me?" she managed to ask.

"Dr. Pearson?" He looked surprised. Pleasantly so. "I think I'm going to regret this."

"Pardon?"

"Never mind. I'm Tyler Marshall."

"Dr. Marshall, what can I do for you?"

"It's Mr. Marshall," he corrected. "I'm an attorney—although this is one time I wish I weren't—and I hope you can do a lot for me."

Amanda was still wearing her white lab coat over a beige denim skirt and sheer blouse. Whoever he was, the man had been assessing her, too, his gaze boldly raking down her body in typical male fashion. The blatant sexuality of his glance was unnerving, while at the same time fascinating and provocative.

"Excuse me?" she said, confused by his statement. His nearness wasn't doing much for her brain function. She suddenly felt lightheaded.

"I hope you can do a lot for me," he repeated. "I apologize for being so forward, but medical school must have been a long, wet experience for your classmates."

Amanda blinked at him. He was gorgeous. His eyes were an incredible shade of blue and his shoulders were so wide they took up the entire doorway. "I don't think I follow."

He laughed. "You're very beautiful, Dr. Pearson. I imagine your colleagues took a lot of cold showers. If I were certain you would treat me, I might even be tempted to be sick."

She laughed, too, although she blushed at the same time. "Being sick isn't much fun. Better develop something minor."

"Like fatigue?" he asked, rolling his shoulders and reaching to massage the back of his neck in a weary gesture. "It's been a long day."

"And a long night," Amanda agreed.

"Very long. In fact, I can't decide which I need the most, a cup of coffee, a hot shower, or a bed."

"Why don't you try all three?" she suggested. "In that order."

"That's an excellent idea, Dr. Pearson. Would you like to join me?" There was a moment's hesitation as he slowly smiled, a charming, lopsided grin. "That is, at least for the coffee."

She had joined him for a lot more than coffee, Amanda thought wryly, getting up from the chair and wandering to the window to glance outside. After she'd refused to testify for him, the magnetism between them had taken over. Then, once she was in love with him, she had started looking at the chart again. One day something had clicked. She had discovered conveniently, right in the middle of the trial, that his client might have had genetic porphyria.

Damn! What was Ty doing here in Rialto? What did he want? He wasn't the type for small towns or small-town cases. He'd as much as admitted that himself. The Whittikers had to be paying him a fortune. Of course, Tommy's father could afford to pay any price to keep his son out of jail. Glenn Whittiker was a multi-millionaire. He owned a commodities trading firm in Chicago and had made a fortune in wheat. During her residency at County Memorial, Amanda had visited the couple several times. Eunice, his wife, who was from Rialto, still had that small-town innocence about her, but Glenn was a wheeler-dealer, in a way, a lot like Ty.

"Mandy?"

The knock on the door roused Amanda from her lethargy and she glanced around, recognizing the voice of her neighbor. Apparently Mrs. Crowley was finished pulling weeds. Whatever could the woman want? Probably to find out about Ty. If the town stuck to its usual pattern, within hours she would be answering enough questions to put on a medical inquisition.

What an unfair presumption. Mrs. Crowley was nosy, but she wasn't obvious and whatever she wanted, it might not have a thing to do with Ty. Amanda was just being testy. The woman would be a welcome diversion. Certainly Amanda didn't need to spend a single moment longer thinking about Tyler Marshall.

"Mandy?" Mrs. Crowley called again. "Are you home, Mandy?"

"Yes, I'm here." Amanda pulled open her kitchen door. Her neighbor stood in the entrance holding a wilted pink petunia. The flower drooped over the edge of the small plastic pot like a tired Alice from Wonderland.

"Goodness you're dirty," the woman remarked.

Amanda laughed and glanced down at her legs. "I think I've regressed back to my childhood."

"You always did like to play in the dirt. Pretty is as pretty does, I always say."

Amanda smiled. Conversation with most of the townspeople was so littered with idioms, and they switched back and forth from one subject to another so quickly, that sometimes she had trouble following, and she'd lived here all her life.

"Yes," she said, not quite sure what she was agreeing to, but agreeing nonetheless. "How's Mr. Crowley's gout?"

"Zeke is just fine, as long as he sticks to his diet. He likes his sweets, though. I found this out front," the older woman went on, indicating the flower. "I thought maybe you overlooked it. You were planting them earlier."

"I had to stop and stitch Jimmy John's finger."

"Is he all right?"

"Just fine," Amanda said.

"Ornery old coot."

"Yes."

"The poor thing's dying."

Amanda hoped they were discussing the flower. "Yes," she repeated, after a moment, taking the petunia from the woman. "Water will probably revive it, though."

"I don't know. It looks pretty sad."

Looking at the blossom, Amanda agreed. It looked sadder than Alice. Sadder than her.

"Why don't we get it into the ground right away," Mrs. Crowley suggested. "I'll be glad to help you."

Amanda didn't feel like planting any more flowers, and although Mrs. Crowley would do anything for her, it was unlike the woman to offer to perform physical labor. She didn't even plant flowers in her own yard. She just had a thing about weeds. "Thank you, Mrs. Crowley, but I think I'll—"

"Nonsense, Mandy," the woman cut in, apparently

anticipating Amanda's refusal. "Come on, now. It'll only take a few minutes to plant this one little flower. I would have done it myself but I didn't know where you wanted to put it."

It was as useless wasting her energy arguing with Mrs. Crowley as it had been thinking about Ty and his reasons for coming to Rialto. Amanda had learned long ago not to quibble with the townspeople over inconsequential issues. They had certain ways of doing things, and they weren't about to change. She'd set about educating them in regard to their medical ailments, and she took a strong stand on things that were important. Planting a petunia was not important.

She followed her neighbor out the door. "Your daddy would be proud of you, Mandy Lou," Mrs. Crowley went on as they headed around the side of the house toward the front. "You've done so much to improve the place."

Although she disagreed regarding her father, Amanda didn't remark. Otis Pearson couldn't have cared less about flowers. The man had loved his patients and would have been equally content to care for them in a vacuum as in a fancy office. When Amanda's mother had been alive, she had been the one to plant flowers. As a child, Amanda could remember the fragrant blossoms in the flower beds, how one bloom had tumbled over the other in a profusion of color and how pretty the yard had appeared. Consequently it was one of the things she'd sworn to do after taking over the office. Until now, she'd been busy modernizing.

"Why ever did you choose pink petunias?"

"No reason." Amanda knelt in the dark, rich soil and started to dig. "I just liked the color."

"Well, I suppose pink is pleasant enough. It'll go with the red brick on your house." Mrs. Crowley handed her the flower. "So tell me about that young man who visited you just a moment ago," she continued as Amanda patted dirt firmly around the foliage. "Handsome devil, he was. You know, Mandy, a nice girl like you ought be thinking of settling down one of these days."

Amanda wanted to laugh. So much for not trusting her own instincts. Obviously, when she'd come over, Mrs. Crowley *had* wanted to discuss Tyler. "I'm happy just the way I am," she answered.

"Has Frank announced his intentions?"

As far as Amanda knew, the town pharmacist was just as content as she to be merely friends. While he was the only eligible bachelor in town, he was much older than Amanda. She'd never even considered them as a couple. "No."

"With Miss Polly gone, folks are going to start thinking of you as the town spinster."

"I'm hardly ancient, Mrs. Crowley." Amanda had just turned thirty recently—not quite decrepit.

But apparently the woman disagreed. "The years pass quickly, my dear. They creep up on you. Not that it's any of my business," she went on, undaunted, "but do I happen to know your visitor?"

Amanda glanced at her neighbor, surprised. "Surely the gossip grapevine hasn't bypassed Elm Street? Are you saying you haven't heard yet?"

Mrs. Crowley pursed her lips disapprovingly. "Amanda, people only gossip because they're concerned."

This time Amanda did laugh. "That's debatable."

Then she shrugged. "The man in question is Gordon Tyler Marshall."

The woman's mouth dropped open. "*The* Gordon Tyler Marshall?"

Amanda nodded. "Yes."

Mrs. Crowley blinked as if she didn't know what to say. "Well," she finally got out, "do you know *his* intentions?"

"He's defending Tommy Whittiker." Amanda supposed it wasn't a secret.

"No, not those intentions," the woman said, frowning. "His intentions toward you."

Amanda hadn't misunderstood. "No," she said, "I'm afraid I don't."

"He is the boy you were messed up with in Chicago, isn't he?"

Boy? Tyler Marshall was hardly a boy. "Yes," Amanda answered. "I dated Ty while I lived in Chicago."

"Has he come to court you?"

"Mrs. Crowley, men don't court women these days."

"Men will always court women, Amanda. Then what does he want?"

Amanda wished she knew the answer. "I told you, he's defending Tommy Whittiker."

Although the woman frowned, it was thoughtful rather than angry. "I'd be willing to bet he's here for some other reason than defending young Tommy."

"I really wouldn't know," Amanda answered.

"You were in love with him."

"Past tense, Mrs. Crowley. That was a long time ago."

"Only two years. Folks around here will remember it

like it was yesterday, Mandy," the old woman said. "Why, I ain't talked to a soul yet and I recall when it happened and how it happened and everything about it. All those Chicago papers were carrying the story, you know. Before you came home your daddy and old Elmer—bless his dearly departed soul—got into a shouting match over who was right, you or Marshall."

Amanda hadn't heard that. "What was the conclusion?"

"Never did come to one. Folks figured it was something only doctors and lawyers could understand. Besides, we were interested in the other matters, like your love affair. You know, Amanda, the heart doesn't think like the head."

Unfortunately. But Amanda didn't want to talk about matters of the heart. And certainly not to Mrs. Crowley. Yet the only way she was going to get out of this situation was to turn the tables on her neighbor. "Speaking of hearts, Mrs. Crowley, didn't you miss your last appointment with me?"

The woman smiled slyly. "I'm on to your tricks, missy. You always try to change the subject when you don't want to talk about something. I've never missed an appointment with my doctor in my life."

"Really? I'd swear you did. Weren't we going to get another electrocardiogram?"

"Huh! You've done enough electrocardiograms on me to wallpaper your office, but yes, you know we were getting another one. My appointment's for next week."

"Great," Amanda said, bending down to gather her garden tools. "I'll see you then. Okay?"

Mrs. Crowley didn't look happy about Amanda

going inside, but there was nothing she could do to prevent it, short of kidnapping her. Apparently the gossip grapevine hadn't failed entirely. The moment Amanda opened her door the telephone started to ring. Most people came right to the point, including her best friend Jean Renee who finally got through an hour later. The two girls had grown up together. When Amanda had gone off to medical school, Jean had run off with her childhood sweetheart. They had eight little children, one for each year they'd been married.

"You've been holding out on me, Amanda," Jean practically gushed. "The man is awesome."

"What happened to 'hello'?"

"Hello. Like I said, the man is awesome."

Amanda sighed. "You've seen Tyler?"

"Yes. At the drugstore. I almost swooned right there in the aisle. Why didn't you warn me, Mandy? He's gorgeous."

Why did everyone persist in telling her how attractive Gordon Tyler Marshall was? She knew exactly how he looked, the texture of his skin, the feel of his hands, the touch of his lips. She shifted uncomfortably and said, "So's the plague. If you're into bacteria."

Jean laughed. "Come on, Amanda. He can't be that bad. What are his intentions?"

Amanda couldn't believe her ears. "Jean, not you, too!"

"Me what?"

Amanda sighed again. "I've just been through that very same conversation with half the town. Frankly, I don't care about Tyler's intentions."

"Ouch," Jean said, "you're sounding awfully bitter."

"What did you expect? You know what he did to me."

Jean paused. "I was never really clear on that, Amanda."

"Dammit, Jean, he used me."

"I thought it was more an argument about ethics."

"Whatever," Amanda conceded. They would never agree. Tyler was right and she was right. And they were both wrong.

"So I guess the heart hasn't grown fonder?" her friend asked.

Amanda nearly groaned aloud. "Jean, please, I've heard enough sayings to last me a lifetime."

Jean chuckled. "Want to come for dinner? It'll get you away from the phone.'

"With your crew?"

"You'll take a pass, huh?"

"Jean, I love your kids, but—"

"You don't have to explain. I eat dinner with them every night. I know what they're like. But if you change your mind, we're having potluck. Just come on out."

They lived on a farm outside of town. Jean's husband had inherited the land and was working hard to make a go of the place. Although things were tough for them financially, they were so in love it sometimes made Amanda uncomfortable to watch them. "Thanks," she said, "but I think I'll turn on the answering machine and catch up on some reading."

"Ugh, I'll take my kids any day to your medical journals."

So would Amanda, really. She was a doctor and that had been her goal for many years, but she also yearned for someone to love her.

"*Mandy?*"

Amanda pulled her attention back to the telephone. "Yes?"

"He's staying, you know."

"Who?"

"Tyler Marshall. He's going to be in town for a while."

But not for long. Even if he was defending Tommy Whittiker, Tyler wouldn't stay in Rialto. Sure, he'd be around town occasionally, after all, the case was an attempted murder. But there wasn't even a nice hotel in Rialto, and Ty simply wasn't the small-town type. More than likely he'd go to Effingham or Lafayette and stay in a fancy suite. Or even Chicago. He could fly back and forth in a private plane. Considering the kind of money he commanded, he could probably buy his own Lear jet. Certainly he could afford to send in researchers, people to do the work for him and merely show up on the court date to defend Tommy. Wasn't that how big-shot lawyers on television handled their cases? She stopped twisting the telephone cord.

"Amanda, are you going to be okay?"

"Sure."

"What are you going to do?"

She shrugged. "Read my medical journals. Fix my head. I hit it on the car hood."

"Did it knock any sense into you? You know, you're not being very smart about this situation."

"Jean, what is it you want from me?"

"For God's sake, Amanda, don't stick your head in the sand."

"I'm not. I'm just not talking about it."

"It. Don't you mean *him*?"

"Him," Amanda corrected.

"All right, suppose you tell me how you're going to accomplish that feat. How are you going to ignore Tyler Marshall?"

"Easy. I intend to avoid him."

"Need I remind you this is a small town? Rialto, Illinois, population twelve hundred."

Small depended on point of view. After fielding all the telephone calls this afternoon, Amanda was certain the town was overpopulated. She had yet to hear from her aunt Sophie. "I'll manage," she answered. "See you later."

"I'll be bringing Danny, Junior, in this week for his checkup."

The child was twenty pounds of destruction. The last time Amanda had examined him, he'd bitten her. "Joy."

Jean laughed as they hung up. "See you then. Hang in there, Mandy."

The phone rang again but Amanda switched it to her machine just in time to intercept her aunt's call. Sophie Pearson would be furious, but Amanda didn't want to talk to another person unless it was medically related.

After taking a long, hot bath, she found a mirror to examine her scalp wound. Ty was right, she could use a couple stitches, but she applied some more antiseptic and sprayed a dressing in place—one of the new innovations she'd bought when the route salesman had come by. If it worked for her, it would work for her patients.

She wandered around the house for the rest of the afternoon and into the night, taking some aspirin for the pain even though she knew it wasn't the treatment of choice—people with skull injuries were supposed to grin and bear it. In her state of mind, she couldn't. She got three more calls from her aunt, but she refused to pick up the phone. She absolutely wouldn't let her mind shift to Tyler Marshall.

She read journal after journal, immersing herself in medicine. Every page she turned reminded her of Ty or of the trial or of the patient she had examined that night in the Emergency Room so long ago. Every page reminded her of diagnosing the genetic illness that had caused the blackout spells, which in turn had generated the trial in the beginning.

Supposedly Jack Cameron had killed his wife by staging an automobile accident and jumping out before the car hit the cement embankment. Because the woman was a Chicago socialite and Jack was from the other side of the tracks, and because there was sex and scandal involved (both parties had been having an affair), the story had been played up in the press and picked up by all the wire services. After reviewing the tests and reading evidence in a journal, Amanda suspected the accident might have occurred because he'd taken a prescription medicine that combined with his illness to cause a blackout spell and was not a result of the vicious rage of which he'd been accused.

But the evidence was flimsy—a couple urine tests and supposition. The illness was something doctors themselves disagreed on, one of those gray areas of medicine that couldn't be proved or disproved depending on who was giving the presentation. Despite her lack of solid facts, toward the end of the trial Ty convinced her to testify for him on the basis of conjecture. It wasn't until afterward that she'd discovered he'd known all along about Jack's medical history, and that he'd led her to that moment of triumph in the courtroom to further his career.

What bothered Amanda the most was that she still wasn't certain whether she'd testified because she was convinced of Jack Cameron's innocence or because she had been in love with Ty. She hadn't dated much as a teenager, and when she went away to medical school she was too busy for men and relationships.

Until Ty. Until that night when she'd met him in the Medical Records Department of County Memorial. He'd made her feel so special, so beautiful—

God, she couldn't think about it. How stupid she'd been! Why hadn't she noticed the chart he was reading, the patient's name? Jack Cameron's father. Why hadn't she realized Ty was using her? Purposely she flipped the magazine page, trying to close her mind to the reminders. Yet there was an article on urine testing and another on drug interactions. And yet another one on diagnosing genetic illnesses. She tried to read a regular magazine, but the first article she turned to was about loving and losing. With a sigh, around midnight, she tossed the magazines aside, turned off the answering machine, and went to bed. Most people in Rialto turned in early, and she wouldn't have any calls this time of night unless it was a true emergency. Maybe if she went to bed she could stop thinking about the man she had loved.

Unfortunately her ploy didn't work. Amanda tossed and turned most of the night, sleeping little. She got up early the next morning and got ready for work, donning a skirt and blouse and a white lab coat. Although she didn't have office hours until later, she had to make rounds at the hospital in Parkersville and she had to see a few of her housebound patients. As a country physician she still made housecalls. Sometimes she felt as though she should have a horse and buggy. Rialto didn't have a hospital, let alone an emergency center, and her patients depended solely on her for medical treatment.

After swallowing some more aspirin for the pain in her head, she perked coffee and took a cup with her into her office. She was dictating a history and physical when the nurse who worked for her opened the front door and came inside. No one in town really knew Inez Bates's age. She was the only nurse in Rialto, and she had worked for Amanda's father for years. At the time she'd been older than him. She was tall and thin and wore her steel-gray hair swept back in a severe bun, and she was one of the few people who didn't call Amanda by her nickname. Perhaps it was due to their careers, the old doctor-nurse syndrome, but they shared a mutual respect based on a strictly professional relationship.

"Good morning, Dr. Pearson," Inez called, breezing through the place carrying the mail in her hand. "I'll just get some coffee and I'll be right back. How are you today?"

"Fine," Amanda called back.

Usually the nurse wasn't much for chitchat, either. Most of the time she was direct and to the point. Coffee in hand, she came into Amanda's office. "I figure you don't want to talk about Tyler Marshall," she said promptly, setting the stage for how they would handle the subject, "so I'll save you the trouble of having to explain. I heard all about it in town, and I don't have an opinion." Without further comment, she held up an envelope. "Lab reports from the hospital. Must be Tommy Whittiker's test results."

Grateful she didn't have to hedge around the subject of Ty all day long, Amanda took the envelope and ripped it open as Inez went into the other room. For a long moment she stared at the results, puzzled, until the intercom buzzing interrupted her.

"Mr. Tyler Marshall on line two," Inez said when Amanda pressed down the button. Uncharacteristically, the woman mumbled, under her breath, "He doesn't waste any time, does he?"

"No, he doesn't," Amanda answered, though she thought better of it. She picked up the telephone. "Ty?"

"Good morning, Dr. Pearson." His tone was cool, clipped, professional. "I was wondering if you had heard anything yet from the lab regarding my client."

But that voice could be soft and seductive, too. Low and husky. Even now the sound of it mesmerized her. It reminded her of nights he had talked to her, called her beautiful, made love to her with that voice. Lord how he'd duped her.

Abruptly Amanda sat forward, willing the memories away. "As a matter of fact, I have the result of Tommy's blood-alcohol level right here," she said.

She read the number to him. There was a long pause. "That's low, isn't it?"

"Yes, it is. In fact, it's almost negligible."

Another long pause. Then all he said was, "Thank you. I'd appreciate it if you could send me a copy of the results right away."

"I'll see to it immediately."

"Later, then."

Amanda hung up before he could say anything more. Not that she thought he would breech their agreement. After her rejection of him yesterday afternoon, he had outlined their relationship quite clearly. Yet she had to admit that she felt a bit disappointed at his impersonal attitude.

Placing the test results inside a manila envelope, she flipped through several other papers before gathering her bag to leave for the hospital. She went into the outer office. Inez was busy on the telephone, and trying to file charts and reports at the same time. The patient billing sat in a corner of the formica counter, long forgotten. Clearly Amanda needed to get some more help. For now though, they'd have to make do until she had some extra cash.

"Inez," Amanda said when the nurse hung up, "I hate to ask you to do this, but can you drop off a copy of Tommy Whittiker's lab results at Mr. Marshall's later today?"

The nurse turned from the file cabinet. "Can't you run it by on your way to Parkersville?"

Amanda didn't want to see Ty. "I'm in a hurry. I'd have to go out of my way."

"Really?" Inez frowned. "He's staying right at the Rialto Arms. Don't you have to pass by on your way out of town?"

"Oh," Amanda said, surprised that he would be there, and that there had been a suitable room available. No one had stayed at the Rialto Arms for years except an occasional out-of-town relative who came for a funeral, or the old vagrants who lived there and paid money on a weekly basis. Now what? "I guess I do. How did you know he's there?"

The nurse smiled. "That was Miss Gertrude on the phone. She's canceled her appointment for this afternoon because she has an important guest—namely one

Gordon Tyler Marshall—and she has to make a boysenberry pie for supper tonight."

"Oh," Amanda said again. "How was her blood pressure last time?"

"Fine," Inez answered. "Don't worry, it'll probably do Miss Gertrude good to swoon over a good-looking man. Might get the blood moving in her system."

At least Miss Gertrude was married, Amanda thought, and didn't have to worry about becoming the town spinster.

"By the way, there are at least ten calls on the machine from your Aunt Sophie."

"I know. I'll call her back later."

"She's coming in for office hours."

"Terrific."

"Say," the nurse went on, missing Amanda's sarcasm, "as long as you're going out, could you swing by the house and check my husband? Ted Bates is sick and he thinks he's dying."

For as long as Amanda had known Inez, the woman had pronounced her husband's name as one word—Tedbates. She never even called him just Ted, always Tedbates. And she seemed so casual about his illness. "What's wrong?" Amanda asked.

"You know men. It's earth-shattering when they're sick. I told him he has the flu, but he doesn't believe me."

Amanda nodded. "I'll be glad to check him."

"See you later, then. I'll hold up things here while you take on the world."

Was that an omen? "Gee, thanks."

"Oh, Dr. Pearson," the nurse said, "just a point of

reference—your young man *is* a hunk. I was quite surprised. Have a good time."

Amanda glared at her nurse. "You know something, Inez? You're all heart."

The nurse grinned. "I know."

So was Tyler Marshall, Amanda thought as she went out the door, only he was all broken heart, and there was no way she was going to get out of having to see him.

Chapter Three

TED BATES WAS FINE. He did have the flu, and all he needed was reassurance that he would survive. If only Tyler Marshall were as simple a matter to dispense with, Amanda thought as she parked her car in front of the Rialto Arms. The engine sputtered and ran on as she shut it off, but she ignored it and concentrated on Ty. After dreaming of him for most of last night, the last thing she needed was to see him. Actually, Amanda had decided that she didn't have to see him. All she had to do was leave the lab results at the desk and have them sent up to him.

But in order to do that she had to go inside the hotel. Here she was, the town physician—the center of gossip—about to enter a building in which the man the entire population knew had been her lover was staying. And everyone had noticed. Up and down the street people had slowed, conversation that had been humming and buzzing stopped, and heads turned to stare at her. Obviously everyone was surprised that she was seeing Ty. So surprised—and staring so intently—that she felt like a heart attack in the midst of cholesterol counters. But she forced a smile and pretended not to notice as she pushed open the door to the ancient hotel.

The Rialto Arms had been built around the turn of the century, and had been modernized several times by several different generations, all with different tastes and purposes in mind. The building was old, with solid, Roman-style architecture on the outside. Rolls of cement and fancy carvings dominated the roof and windows. A huge marble lion served sentry beside the double doors, the once-beautiful white stone stained and pitted by the elements. Inside, layers of paint peeled from the walls and the place was as musty as an old attic. Mr. Sam, Miss Gertrude's husband, sat behind the typical oak desk, on which a pot of flowers had been placed in imitation of fancy hotels. But the pot was an old chamberpot, speckled blue and white like a bird's egg, and the flowers were red plastic roses saved from a bygone era.

Noting it all, and excusing it because, despite some unhappy moments, she loved this town and its inhabitants, Amanda stepped forward.

Mr. Sam ignored her. But the townsfolk looking in the window didn't; she couldn't help but notice three-quarters of the population had congregated around the hotel, waiting to see what she would do. Finally, she banged the bell.

"Why, Mandy Lou," the old man looked up and said in total feigned innocence, "whatever brings you here to the Rialto Arms?" He lowered his voice and quirked an eyebrow. "You must have heard about our honored guest."

Honored guest? One would think he was referring to the King of Siam. Amanda nodded as she held out the lab results. "Yes, I have. If you don't mind I'd like to leave this envelope for Mr. Marshall. Be sure and have Miss Gertrude make another appointment with my office. Whether or not you have honored guests, we need to keep an eye on her blood pressure."

"Now, Mandy, you know Miss Gertrude wouldn't dare skip another appointment with you," he said. "She's well-aware of how important it is to see her doctor. But she has to bake a pie for Mr. Marshall. He's expecting dinner tonight."

Amanda paused. "Can't Mr. Marshall eat at the café?"

"Oh, no." Sam's eyes widened in horror, as though the mere thought were a sacrilege. "He rented a suite, Mandy, and when you rent a suite at the Rialto Arms, meals are included. It's part of the price. An' he paid for it for a whole month in advance. Speaking of food," he went on, looking her up and down, "wouldn't hurt you to have a little breakfast. You're looking a mite peaked these days, Doc."

"I'm fine."

"Can't prove it by me. I do declare, you're lookin' peaked. Why even your ribs are showin'."

Petunias weren't important, Amanda reminded herself. She placed the lab results on the desk. "If you'll please give this to Mr. Marshall."

Mr. Sam frowned as he stared at the envelope. "Them's Tommy Whittiker's lab results?"

"Yes."

"Them's important, right?"

"Yes."

"An' confidential?"

"That's right," Amanda said, swooping the envelope back up. Although Mr. Sam and Miss Gertrude had probably listened to every word of her conversation with Ty this morning, and knew more than she did about the results, she was better off delivering the envelope herself. At least it would reach him without being steamed open. "I'd better take it up myself. Could you tell me what room he's in?"

"Presidential Suite," Mr. Sam announced proudly. "Whole top floor. Goes for fifty dollars a night."

Amanda didn't remark on the price. She glanced at the steps, which were rickety-looking, even from here. If she remembered correctly, the Presidential Suite was three flights up.

"Take the elevator if you want," Mr. Sam said after a moment.

Amanda turned her gaze to the ancient elevator. It looked more rickety than the steps. "I think I'll stick to the stairs."

"Well, choice is yours. I'll let Mr. Marshall know you're on your way, so's he can expect you. Miss Gertrude is up there, right now, serving breakfast. If'n you're gonna want some coffee you better tell me now, so's you can bring up a cup with you. Miss Gertrude won't want to have to make another trip up, you know. Exercise ain't exactly her forte."

"Can't she take the elevator?"

"Help don't take the elevator. That's reserved for guests."

"Oh," Amanda answered. Of course. How logical.

"Well, you needn't worry, Mr. Sam. I won't be staying. I'm just dropping off the test results."

"Yup. Sure. That's what they all say, then pretty soon they start talkin' and they sit down, and then they want a cup of coffee and then—"

"She has to make another trip," Amanda cut in, "and exercise isn't her forte. Right. I know."

Forcing a smile, she started to walk away, but Mr. Sam called to her. "By the way, Amanda," he said, as though the thought had just struck him, "I hope you don't think we're traitors, Miss Gertrude and me, 'cause we're housing Mr. Marshall. He paid us money, you know, and we are in business."

What an odd thing to say. She frowned. "Yes, I know. What are you getting at, Mr. Sam?"

"Jest that we don't want you to think that we've abandoned you. You're the hometown girl and Mr. Marshall's the stranger, even if he is defending Tommy. If it came to a choice, we'd take you over him any day, paying customer or not."

"In other words you and Miss Gertrude are going to rally round me?"

"If'n you want us to. Whole town would if'n you needed us. Jest wanted you to know that."

Sometimes there were advantages to living in a small town. "Thanks," she said, amused and yet at the same time touched by his sincerity, "but you needn't worry, Mr. Sam. I can hold my own."

"Even with Mr. Marshall?"

She nodded. "Even with Mr. Marshall."

The stairs creaked with every step Amanda took, sounding like something out of a horror chamber. But they held. Actually they were probably sturdier than they looked, she told herself. The hotel had to pass an annual safety inspection. She remembered because the last time the inspector had come around, Miss Gertrude had gotten so anxious her blood pressure had shot out of control. It had taken a week to bring it down.

The Presidential Suite had to have been one of the renovations made in the early twenties. At the top of the third flight of steps, Amanda came to a foyer that had been blocked out with wallboard. Illuminated only by a crystal light fixture that had seen better days, the area was so dark she could hardly see. Looking closer, she managed to make out pictures of presidents that lined the walls on either side, obviously cut from a school book and pasted onto cardboard. Directly ahead, double oak doors opened into the room. She picked up the ornate brass door knocker crafted in the shape of a gavel and rapped twice.

Miss Gertrude answered. She was a short, plump lady in her late sixties, and she wore her gray hair knotted on top of her head with wide white combs sticking out from the bun. For as long as Amanda had known the woman she had worn a bib apron over her clothes, and today was no exception. It was just fancier than usual.

"Well, hello, Mandy Lou," she said in greeting, obviously enjoying her role as hostess to the honored guest. "Fancy seeing you here. Mr. Marshall is expecting you."

"Thank you." Amanda inclined her head as the woman swung the door wider, allowing her to step inside.

At least the place was brighter inside. Sunshine streamed through the heavily draped windows, spotlighting the dust that floated hazily through the air. The decor was still presidential. More pictures lined the walls, and the wallpaper carried out the gavel theme. A canopied bed had been plopped in the middle of the room, looking lonely and swallowed up by the other furnishings: a heavy oak dresser, a tall armoire, several overstuffed chairs done in a dusky rose pattern, and a huge cherrywood desk at which Ty sat, papers, books, and legal briefs spread out in front of him.

As usual he looked better than any man had a right to appear at any time, let alone early in the morning. He was wearing light gray suitpants and a long-sleeved white shirt. His jacket was on the bed and his tie hung loose around his neck, as though he'd been too busy to bother with it yet. His shirt was unbuttoned at the neck, revealing a smattering of thick hair that matched the dark, unruly curls on his head. How many times had she run her hands through his hair? Spread her palm across his chest?

"Good morning, Dr. Pearson," he said in that slow, liquid-velvet voice.

Amanda jerked her gaze from his chest and stood stiffly in the middle of the room. "Mr. Marshall."

"Would you like a cup of coffee, Mandy Lou?" Miss Gertrude asked, bustling past her.

Amanda glanced at the cart standing to one side, much of the food untouched. Ty had never cared for breakfast. "No, thank you. I'll pass."

"Are you sure?" the old woman went on. "I could have Mr. Sam bring you up a cup. Exercise ain't exactly his forte, but it would do him good to walk a mite now and then."

The couple were of a like mind. But Amanda shook her head. "I really don't have time for coffee."

"Oh, that's right. You're always so busy. Well, then, I guess I'll be going." She turned to smile and wave at Tyler. "Toodeloo."

Ty winked at her. "Thanks for breakfast."

When the door closed, he glanced at Amanda. He had leaned back in the chair, his head resting on his hands and his feet stretched before him. "Sure you won't have some coffee?" he offered again, gesturing to the pot. "I could get a glass from the bathroom."

"No," she said. "I'm in a hurry."

"All right."

Amanda shifted uneasily. She should just give him the laboratory results and leave. But for some reason her feet felt rooted to the floor and her tongue to her mouth. Why couldn't she speak? All she had to say was *I loved you so damned much. Why did you hurt me?*

God, she could hardly blurt that out.

Ty finally came to the point. "Is that a copy of Tommy Whittiker's blood-alcohol level?" he asked, nodding to the envelope in her hand.

"Yes." Because there didn't seem to be any other convenient way to give him the papers, she stepped forward and handed him the envelope, being very careful not to touch him. If he noticed, he didn't remark.

"What do you think?" he asked.

"About what?"

"The results."

Presuming Miss Gertrude hadn't left, but was listening outside the door, Amanda glanced toward the hall and pitched her voice low. "I suspect the walls have ears."

Tyler shrugged. "It doesn't matter. Eventually the lab tests will become a matter of public record anyhow."

"Then as I told you on the telephone," she said, "the results were low."

"That means Tommy wasn't drinking."

"I think that's a safe assumption." She paused. "Although he could have had a beer several hours before. Whatever alcohol he drank, most of it was detoxified from his system by the time we drew his blood."

Ty had opened the envelope to study the square yellow sheet of paper. Then he glanced at Mandy. "You know this makes Tommy look even more suspect."

She nodded. "Yes, I know."

"The prosecution will say he willfully ran down the Martin boy."

What could she say? "They did argue."

"That doesn't make him guilty of murder."

"Look, Ty," she said at last, "I didn't come here to argue with you about Tommy Whittiker. I'm sorry the results weren't what you had expected, but I didn't have anything to do with it. I'm just giving you a copy of the numbers."

He sighed as he tossed the papers aside and ran a hand wearily through his hair. "I know. I'm sorry, too." In one quick motion he stood and walked to the cart to pour himself some more coffee. "Frankly, I'm not sure what I had hoped the results would show," he went on after a moment. "For some crazy reason I didn't want Tommy to be proven drunk."

"It looks like you got your wish." Amanda hadn't meant to sound flippant, and thankfully Ty didn't take her remark that way.

He sat down again. "I sure did. Tell me, is Bobby Martin still sedated?" At her surprised expression, he said, "I called the hospital yesterday. The charge nurse explained to me that he was under sedation and that you were the physician of record."

Amanda nodded. "Yes, I am his doctor." She was everyone's doctor. "If he's still stable when I get to the hospital today I'll be taking him off the critical list."

"Then I can talk to him?"

"After Sheriff Toombs."

"Fine."

"Have you spoken with Tommy Whittiker?" He had been given bond and as soon as she discharged him from the hospital, he was supposed to go back to stay with his grandparents.

"Once. Shortly. I'm seeing him again this afternoon. Then I need to talk with his girl friend."

There wasn't much more to say. Amanda glanced around the room wondering again why he had come here, why he had taken this particular case, why he was staying at the Rialto Arms. The words came out before she could stop them. "What are you trying to prove, Ty?"

Glancing at her, he said, "A kid's innocence."

She knew he hadn't meant to sound flippant either. "No. Here." She gestured around the room at the bed, the gray peeling wallpaper, the dingy upholstery. "What are you trying to prove by staying here? This isn't your style."

He followed her gaze and shrugged. "I've lived in worse."

"Not lately."

"Am I supposed to apologize for that?"

"No."

"Good, because I don't intend to. Believe it or not, I work hard for my money, Mandy." He paused for the briefest of moments. "Do you remember my apartment?"

How could she forget? The first time he'd taken her there they'd made love. He'd cooked her dinner. They'd laughed over spaghetti and meatballs and had toasted each other with cheap wine. Later, lying in front of a picture of a roaring fire and pretending it was a fireplace, he'd kissed her. Then he'd made love to her—slow, delightful, delicious love. She had been charmed by him, and by the quaintness of his third floor walk-up, rattling pipes and all. She'd laughed when he'd teased about the size of the cockroaches crowding his kitchen, and about becoming friends with the area mice. But he wasn't teasing when he'd told her that one day he planned to be rich enough to buy and sell Nelson Rockefeller.

"Do you remember, Mandy? I do." She glanced up when she realized he had moved beside her. His breath feathered onto her hair, curling up her neck. "I remember every moment we spent together, the feel of you in my—"

Quickly she moved away. She wasn't charmed anymore. "Yes, I remember, too, Ty. I remember how you wanted to be rich. I remember how you wanted to win that case."

"I want to win all my cases, Amanda."

"I didn't put it together then, but once you told me if you won the Jack Cameron case you would get that New York job. And you'd have fame and fortune. You wanted it all so badly, Ty. Do you remember that?"

"Yes."

She laughed bitterly. "God, I was stupid. I didn't even put it together when I testified for you."

"I didn't ask you to testify so I could get rich, Amanda, or for the job or for any other reason except that I believed in Jack Cameron's innocence."

"And what about us, Ty? Did you believe in us?"

"We were in love."

"That was two years ago." A lifetime ago.

"Mandy..."

"Please call me Dr. Pearson," she said, catching herself starting to soften. She moved toward the door. She couldn't be near him any longer. She had to get away. But she paused with her hand on the knob and turned back. "By the way, Miss Gertrude has high blood pressure. Since you seem determined to stay in Rialto, I'd appreciate it if you could be easy on her. I don't want her climbing up and down the steps to wait on you."

"I am staying, Amanda," he answered.

She nodded. "So I gather."

She opened the door to leave, managing a tricky sidestep when the elderly woman tumbled into the room headfirst. Obviously Amanda's earlier suspicion that the woman was listening had been accurate.

"Miss Gertrude."

"Why, Amanda," the woman said, finally righting herself, "you shouldn't open doors so fast, dear. Likely to leave a body lying on the floor. Are you going already? I was just fixing to ask Mr. Marshall if he wanted a nice glass of lemonade. I made him some last night after Jimmy John told us he had a hankering for it, and he just loved it."

Ty smiled. "It was very good. Did you come all the way upstairs just to ask me if I wanted a glass of lemonade? I'm flattered."

Miss Gertrude beamed. "You're so charming, Mr.

Marshall. Don't you think he's charming, Amanda?"

Next he'd charm the town.

"Yes," Amanda agreed, suddenly furious with him for encouraging the old lady. "But he drinks too much lemonade. None today. My orders."

Miss Gertrude looked stunned; her mouth had dropped open in an expression of disbelief. "Gracious, Dr. Pearson. Since when is lemonade harmful?"

"Since now," Amanda answered. "Too much acid. And I will see you later today," she went on to insist. "Boysenberry pie or not, I expect you to keep your appointment. Be there for office hours this afternoon."

"But I—"

"Be there."

Amanda didn't wait to listen to objections. Tossing her purse over her shoulder, she marched out the door and down the steps. When she reached the bottom landing, and noticed all the people who had gathered inside the hotel, waiting for a tidbit of gossip, she paused and called up, "And don't forget to tell everyone how he ravished me."

Then, smiling at Mr. Sam, whose mouth became a twin of his wife's, she walked across the lobby and out into the bright, sunshiny day.

Since traffic was light, Amanda arrived in Parkersville in less than half an hour. It was located between Senton and Rialto, and enemy towns or not, that's where all sick people had to go for treatment. Every once in a while she had to take calls at the hospital, and the night of the accident she'd been the doctor of record. That's how Bobby had become her patient. Thankfully, today she didn't have any more car trouble.

The engine wheezed once or twice, but that was all. She practically flew over the country roads. Maybe it had been good to change the water pump.

Sheriff Toombs was waiting at the hospital for her. He was a big man, made bigger by his khaki-colored uniform, Smokey-the-Bear police hat, and heavy tin badge. He leaned against the nurses station counter, tapping his foot impatiently. "Mandy Lou, I been waitin' here for you nigh on to an hour," he said the moment she stepped out of the elevator and into the ICU. "Inez told me you was comin' to the hospital."

"I had to drop off some lab results, Sheriff Toombs. What can I do for you?"

"First of all, you can stop foolin' around with that city slicker of yours and come take care of your patient."

Amanda paused and said, "Pardon me?"

The sheriff sighed. "I'm itchin' to talk to Bobby Martin, and I'm beginnin' to think you're stonewallin' my efforts," he went on.

"Stonewalling?" Amanda saw every color of the rainbow. Was he accusing her of obstructing justice?

"Yes, ma'am, stonewalling." At least he turned as red as she felt; a ruddy flush stained his throat and face. "I'm sorry, Doc, but you been puttin' me off and puttin' me off. Now I aim to see that boy today, and ask him all about how Tommy Whittiker run him down on the motorsickle. 'Scuse me," he said to an aide who went out around the corner wheeling a sphygmomanometer beside her. "Sorry."

"Wait a minute, Sheriff Toombs," Amanda said, suddenly oblivious to the personnel bustling around them, "aren't you making a pretty strong presumption here?"

Not to mention his accusation regarding her. She didn't know much about law, but she'd learned enough from Ty to know that the sheriff was violating the principles of justice. "What if Tommy didn't run Bobby down?"

The sheriff just shook his head. "Everybody knows he done did it, Mandy. That don't mean we like it. Now I know that in a manner of speaking the Whittiker boy is from Rialto, and we like to protect our own, but heck, he even admits to it. What's a body supposed to do? We got to prosecute him." He stood tall and the veins in his neck stuck out as he added, "But you're not lettin' us see the intended victim."

Amanda drew a deep breath. There ought to be a medical school course in patience, particularly for small-town physicians. Because he was so naive it was hard to be angry at the man. "What about a trial, Sheriff Toombs?"

"What about it?"

She gritted her teeth. "Don't you need a trial to convict Tommy Whittiker?"

"Why, sure, Mandy," he answered. "We got to have a trial. Lordie, you know that. I was gonna ask you to testify."

Amanda kept trying to hold onto logic. "Don't you think the county prosecutor should be the one to ask me to testify, Sheriff Toombs? And shouldn't he be here when you question Bobby Martin?"

"Yeah, sure." The man nodded. "He's comin'. Got a few things to do first, though. I told him I'd get Bobby's statement."

Terrific. "I'm afraid you're going to have a hard time doing that," Amanda told him. "Bobby's still sedated."

The sheriff frowned. "You wouldn't be foolin' me,

would you, Mandy? You wouldn't be maneuverin' to let your city slicker in here first so's he could talk Bobby out of tellin' what really happened? That boy's been sedated a long time, over three days now."

Amanda stood with the chart half open and counted to twenty. A nurse passed by, glancing at them. Amanda continued counting to twenty-five. "That boy's been *sick* a long time," she finally said. "Must I remind you, Sheriff Toombs, that Robert Martin has been critically ill?"

"Huh, well, that's true enough, I suppose."

"Then what's the problem?"

Uncomfortable, he shifted back and forth again, his face a bright ruddy red. "Now, Mandy."

"Out with it," she said. "What's the problem?"

He glanced at her sheepishly. "I just never figured you'd be the type to be in collusion with someone, Mandy Lou. Not you."

She didn't follow the supposition. "Whatever makes you think I'm in collusion with someone, Sheriff?"

"You're seein' that lawyer fella, ain't ya? That stranger. Ya went with him in Sheecago."

What did that have to do with now? "Sheriff Toombs, please be assured that I am not *seeing* Tyler Marshall. He came to my office yesterday to look at Tommy Whittiker's records and I dropped off some lab results to him this morning. And even if I were seeing him," she went on testily, "I'm a physician, and I'm able to keep my professional and personal lives separate."

"You testified for him once and you were goin' with him then. You were lovers."

Amanda reddened. How did she explain that? Obviously she hadn't been able to keep her personal and professional lives separated at that time. "Yes, I did." Placing the chart on the counter, she pulled her stethoscope from her pocket. "Tell you what, Sheriff Toombs, why don't you go in the room with me and you can see for yourself that Bobby is sedated and unable to answer your questions for the time being."

The sheriff stared at her. "It ain't that I don't believe you, Doc."

"Then are you questioning my motives?"

"I ain't exactly doin' that neither," he said. "I'm just worried. Cain't get caught with my pants down, you know. I'm the sheriff and this is my town. Folks been saying that Marshall feller is one slick dude."

So this whole episode had been a matter of professional pride. Fear of one-upmanship. Amanda nodded. "I understand. Truthfully, Sheriff Toombs, Bobby Martin is unable to speak with you. I'm hoping to take him off the critical list today, though, and you should be able to interview him in the morning. I assure you personally that Tyler Marshall won't get near his room in the meantime. How's that?"

The man beamed. "Why, that's perfect, Doc. I'll be able to get the prosecutor here and everything."

Amanda smiled, too. "Great. Now, if you'll excuse me."

"How you gonna do it?"

She turned back to him. "How am I going to do what?"

"Keep Marshall away. Folks say he's pretty persistent."

Seemingly folks said a lot about Tyler. But that was

true. He clung on tenaciously. "Yes, he is persistent," Amanda admitted.

"Folks say he not only wants to win this case, they say he's after you."

Too bad Sheriff Toombs didn't know Tyler's real intentions. "That's ridiculous. After me for what?"

Sheriff Toombs shook his head sadly. "For all your schoolin', Mandy Lou, you sure don't know nothin' about men. Marshall's *after* you."

Men was another course they didn't teach in medical school. She frowned. "What do you mean? What are people saying about me and Ty?"

"Folks don't have to say it to be true, Mandy. It's plain to see. Man's like a bloodhound, hot on your trail. Why I wouldn't be surprised to see him here any second now, steppin' right through that elevator door."

"That's ridiculous."

"Ya said that already."

"Because it's true. The entire thing is ridiculous. Tyler Marshall is not hot on my trail."

"Yup, he is. You just cain't recognize it. Or don't want to. One or the other. And folks say he's liable to get both. He's gonna win his case and get you, too."

What had happened to the town rallying around her? "Really, now?" Amanda retorted, growing angrier by the minute. She'd always had such a hard time controlling her temper. "I don't suppose you'd care to place a little wager on that fact?"

"You fixin' to bet with me?" he asked incredulously.

"Yes," she said. "Afraid to lose?"

"Me, afraid? Why, I ain't never been afraid of nothing in my life, 'cept maybe as a youngin'. Only I don't understand, why would I want to bet with ya?"

Amanda pursed her lips. "To prove a point."

Just then the elevator doors opened and Tyler Marshall stepped out. As usual he was impeccably groomed. He'd donned his jacket and knotted his tie which was hooked by a pearl stud. The snowy white cuffs of his shirt peeked exactly three-quarters of an inch from his sleeves. He was carrying a briefcase of rich, brown leather. "Good morning, Dr. Pearson," he said. "Sheriff Toombs. Fancy meeting you here."

Amanda stared at him dumbfounded.

"Yes, fancy that." Smiling in amusement, Jediah Toombs raised himself to his full height, hitched his pants up over his ample abdomen, and winked at her. "See what I mean? My mama didn't raise no fool, Mandy Lou Pearson. You got yourself a wager."

Chapter Four

"WHAT WAGER?"

Ty looked genuinely puzzled. Of course he would be, he had no idea what she and Sheriff Toombs were talking about. But Amanda was furious anyhow, with both men. It was bad enough that the sheriff was teasing her and that Tyler contributed to her chagrin by following her around and flashing his damned sexy smile. The man should be arrested for deceptive advertising.

"None of your business," she snapped as she marched down the hall to Bobby Martin's room. Maybe Sheriff Toombs would be jealous enough to choke Ty in the meantime.

As she had since the accident, Tommy's girlfriend, Sandy Samuels, sat at Bobby's bedside. Amanda spent a few moments talking with her, knowing how she felt being the center of gossip. She was young, though, and resilient, and Amanda had faith that she would come through this crisis a stronger person.

Ten minutes later, when she came out of the room, Ty and Sheriff Toombs were laughing and talking like old war buddies. So much for one-upmanship. Surprising everyone by slamming the chart down on the counter, Amanda headed for the elevator and the next floor.

"What'd ya suppose got into her?" Sheriff Toombs muttered aloud.

"You got me," she heard Ty answer. "I'm afraid women aren't my forte."

Amanda burned with fury.

Because of their attitudes, and because Tommy and Bobby really *were* too sick to talk much, she didn't allow either man to see either of her patients that day. After examining both Bobby and Tommy, she continued her order prohibiting visitors, except for immediate family. Still ignoring Ty and Sheriff Toombs, absolutely furious with them, she finished her rounds and stalked out of the hospital. Ty's Mercedes was parked out front, and so was the one squad car the town of Rialto possessed. For one fleeting, vengeful moment she thought about deflating the tires, but better judgment intruded, and she got in her own car and drove away.

She quickly made rounds of her housebound patients and got back to her office just in time for hours. She didn't think much on the call from Frank as she walked in the door—he was a pharmacist and he could be checking on a prescription she had ordered. But Inez grinned when she mentioned that Aunt Sophie was in an examining room.

Amanda was in for a grilling. She took the call first. Frank did check on a prescription and then he asked, "Are we still on for dinner tonight? I thought we'd go over to Effingham and get some catfish."

God, she had forgotten. "I'm sorry, Frank, I've got so much to do tonight."

"Are you sure that's the reason?"

"Of course," she answered. "Why do you doubt me?"

"I've been hearing about your lawyer friend all over town."

At least Frank was honest. Amanda hoped she could be as open. "Have you been hearing about me and him?"

"No, just him."

"Ty and I broke up a long time ago, Frank."

"But do you still care for him?"

Open, she reminded herself, and honest. "I'm afraid that even if I did care for him too much happened between us to patch it up."

"Folks say that from what they can figure, he seems to be a nice fella. I know I'm not much of a catch, Amanda."

How sad for him to feel that way. Amanda was at a loss for words. She didn't want to lead him on. She didn't want to hurt him, either. If he was leading up to something she'd have to break off with him soon. "Frank, I didn't think our relationship was serious. Is it?"

"I don't know. Maybe we could discuss it."

"That's a good idea."

"How about the town picnic next week? I'll bid for your lunch and we can spend the day talking."

"Great."

"You will be there?"

"Yes, I'm coming." She didn't have much choice. Everyone went to the town picnic. There were games and booths and a carnival. It was a day of celebration and there were no "bah humbugs" allowed.

"See you then."

"Sure." Amanda hung up the phone and headed toward the examining room. And her aunt.

Sophie Pearson wasn't as easy to deal with. Like everyone else, she wanted to know Tyler's intentions. And Amanda's intentions. And Frank's intentions. Amanda wished she had a crystal ball, for she wanted the answer to those things just as badly as everyone else.

She was saved from a lengthy inquisition only by her other patients who were waiting to be examined. By the time she had fielded all their questions and treated all their ailments, she was exhausted. She wanted nothing more than to fall into bed and sleep the night away. However, she still had to call the hospital and check on Tommy and Bobby, and more lab reports were waiting for her attention.

Fleetingly she thought of Ty, of him standing there at the hospital desk with Sheriff Toombs. Would he be angry at her for not allowing the sheriff to see Bobby Martin?

No matter, she'd done what she had to do.

Two hours later Amanda was going through the last of the laboratory reports. She got to Tommy Whittiker's name and paused. It was just a routine blood test, nothing special, not a single chemistry out of kilter. As she'd mentioned to Ty, he was a healthy teenager. But something about the report bothered her.

Actually, she admitted, something about him bothered her, or rather it was the case that bothered her. She was certain there had been plenty of times that someone had gone crazy and went on a killing rampage, but generally speaking, nice people didn't try to kill their friends, and despite everything, Tommy Whittiker was nice. But how was Ty going to prove that? Or would he? She sighed and placed the lab report in the file. Thank goodness it wasn't up to her.

Amanda slept well that night. She only dreamed of Ty once, and she managed to wake up and put him out of her mind. The next morning she was greeted by another stack of lab reports. Inez had come in with the mail and tossed it on her desk. "Where are all these things coming from?" she muttered, sifting through page after page of reports.

"I believe you ordered them," Inez answered. "Or else they wouldn't be here. Don't you need them? Insurance companies would be glad to hear that. So would all our patients, for that matter."

Amanda glared at her nurse. "I don't order unnecessary tests." She just had several people in the hospital, and things tended to accumulate. She nodded to the papers in Inez's hand. "What are those?"

"Tommy Whittiker's blood chemistries. I got them out of his file. Mr. Marshall called and wanted to know if we'd gotten back anything else."

"Ty called?" For some crazy reason Amanda's heart hit the ground. She hadn't heard the phone, and to her disgust, she realized she'd been waiting for it. For all her bluster, she'd wanted him to call. "When?"

"This morning. You were making coffee. I thought you might go by the Rialto Arms again and drop them off to him."

"But there's nothing significant in his report. Everything was normal."

"He wants them anyhow."

"All right." Amanda took the reports. Why fight it? Actually she owed Ty an explanation for yesterday, and she was going to yell at Miss Gertrude for not showing up for her examination. High blood pressure was nothing to fool around with.

"See you this afternoon," Inez called as Amanda went out the door. "And don't order anything you don't want to see."

Amanda just nodded.

Summers could be sweltering in Rialto, and today promised to be one of the hotter days of the season. Since it was situated close to the Little Wabash River, which meandered through the outskirts of the southern Illinois town, the humidity was usually high, too. Before she got into her car Amanda pulled off her lab coat and tossed it on the passenger seat. By the time she got to the hospital she might sweat to death. She didn't dare run the air-conditioning, not with her car on the fritz. She was just glad when the engine started.

She had almost arrived at the Rialto Arms when she noticed Ty out in front of an old house on the next block. At first she wasn't certain it was him. Gordon Tyler Marshall dressed in jeans and sweat, pounding nails into a rickety porch? She'd never seen him in anything except a suit, and the only physical labor he'd ever performed had been in a bed—unfortunately it had been her bed. Amanda slowed the car and looked back, but it was definitely Ty, stripped to the waist and working diligently. What in the world was he doing?

She asked him that exact question when she parked the car and walked up the drive.

"Well, good morning, Amanda," he answered, flashing his slow, sexy grin. He placed the hammer aside and grabbed a rag to wipe the sweat from his face. "Fancy meeting you—"

"Don't," she cut in.

He just grinned wider. "Don't you like colloquial expressions?"

"No."

"All right then, how are you today?"

Amanda stared at him as though he'd lost his mind. "Fine."

"I see you have some more lab reports for Tommy," he went on, reaching out to take the papers from her hand. "Anything significant?"

"No. Nothing. What are you doing, Ty?"

"What do you mean?"

"I mean, what are you doing?" She gestured around at the house. "What are you doing here pounding nails in an old porch?"

"I'm hanging up a sign," he said, holding up a fancy wooden plate with his name carved inside.

"For what?"

"To advertise my trade, of course. I've bought the place." Now he gestured around. "Don't you like it? I figure I can have it renovated and completely furnished in a couple weeks, so I'm hanging up a sign to tell the town I'm a lawyer, and that I'm accepting clients. What do you think?"

Amanda thought so much she could hardly speak.

She practically choked with rage. "You've bought this house?" she said incredulously. "You closed on a house in one day? How? What the hell for?"

"It was empty," he explained. "As I understand it, the people who used to live here have moved. I paid cash. The bank had the title, and I took possession of it this morning. I bought the place because I've reconciled myself to the fact that I'm going to be here for a while and I need somewhere comfortable to stay. " He flashed another grin. "Okay?"

"No," she said, shaking her head. "No, it's not okay. You don't want to live here, Ty. This is Rialto, Illinois, population twelve hundred. Why are you doing this?"

"I told you I need to stay somewhere comfortable."

"There are hundreds of hotels in this state. You didn't have to buy a home. What are you trying to prove? And you're going to do the carpentry work yourself?" she went on. "That's ludicrous."

"Why? I'm fairly decent with my hands." His remark made her flush, but he didn't seem to notice. "I put myself through law school building houses."

That explained his physique, Amanda thought. Odd that he hadn't mentioned that to her before—of course their affair had been brief. Actually she knew very little about him, where he came from, what his childhood was like, what he wanted from life—except for notoriety.

"And I've got nothing else to do," he went on. "Since I can't see my client, I have to keep busy."

She flushed again. She knew she owed him an explanation. "Ty, I didn't write that no-visitors order to get back at you."

He smiled. "Yes, you did, but that's all right. I told

you, I've already reconciled myself to the fact that I'm going to be here for a long time. And it won't hurt my case or either boy to rest one more day. Tell me, though, what got you so upset?"

"Nothing." Nothing important, that is.

"That's not like you, Amanda. Usually you're more in control."

Darn the man! Where did he get his audacity? "It's really not your concern whether I'm in or out of control," she snapped. "I told you yesterday I want to keep our relationship strictly professional—and that does not include conjecture in regard to my behavior."

"My, you are in a tizzy."

"Who said I was in a tizzy?" That was a word Tyler would never have used.

"Sheriff Toombs. Said you had a terrible stubborn streak." He paused. "Of course, I already knew that. I found out two years ago how stubborn you can be."

She glared at him. He went from bad to worse. "It sounds as though you and the sheriff had a nice little chat."

"We did. He's a very interesting man."

Interesting was an odd way to describe Sheriff Toombs. "What else did you talk about?"

"This and that. Actually, it was the sheriff who told me about the house for sale. I came right over and put the money down." He frowned. "Why are you so upset? Didn't you tell me not to overwork Miss Gertrude?"

"Wasn't she upset that you left the Rialto Arms?"

"No, she's quite amenable," he said, "particularly since I donated the money to name a suite after me. She insisted on baking another boysenberry pie for me. I couldn't convince her otherwise."

"Ty, please don't make fun of the people here."

"I'm not," he said, and from the sound of his voice she knew he was being sincere. "I'm just trying to fit in."

"What about when you leave Rialto?"

"What about it?"

He knew what she meant. He would ingratiate himself into the community and then leave without a backward glance. Which was fine in normal circumstances. In a small town like Rialto people would feel betrayed. Like she felt betrayed. She shook her head. "I keep asking you, Ty, why are you doing this?"

"And I guess I don't understand what you're getting at, Amanda. Doing what?"

"Trying to ingratiate yourself in my community."

"I'm visiting people, being friendly."

"Somehow, that doesn't strike me as being ethical. You're here for a case."

"Just because I'm representing a client accused of murder, I can't chat with people?"

"You know what I mean, Ty."

"No, Amanda," he said, "I don't. Suppose you explain."

She sighed. "You're trying to worm your way in here and deceive people."

"Being friendly is deceptive? Mandy, I think you have things mixed up. I'm here to represent Tommy Whittiker. At the same time I'm getting to know the townsfolk. Believe me, that's not a crime."

"Maybe not in your mind."

"What do you want from me, Amanda?"

"I want you to go away."

He glanced down at the papers in his hand. "I will,

as soon as I clear Tommy Whittiker of murder." All of a sudden he glanced back at her. "Amanda, how do you feel about him?"

What a strange question. "Tommy? Why?"

"Do you like him?"

"Yes, he's a nice boy."

"If it came down to it, would you testify for him?"

She didn't understand. "About what? A low blood-alcohol level? There's nothing to testify for."

He paused thoughtfully. "Maybe. Maybe not. I guess we'll have to wait and see."

"I guess. Excuse me," she said, hitching her purse over her shoulder, "I have to go. I need to get to the hospital."

He gestured toward the house. "Sure you won't come in for a minute? I could show you around."

Said the spider to the fly. That was all she needed, to go into his house, right here on Main Street with the entire community watching. "No, thanks."

"Oh, Mandy—" He called to her as she started to walk away.

She turned around, pausing. "Dr. Pearson."

He smiled tolerantly. "Sorry, I keep forgetting. *Dr. Pearson*. You'll let me know if you get any more lab results on Tommy?"

"Of course."

"And when I can see Bobby Martin?"

"Certainly."

"Have a good day." Then he grinned that damned sexy smile and picked up the hammer.

It wasn't so much as what he said, but the way he said it that made Amanda angry. Damn the man! She was so furious she clenched her teeth together. Did he know how upset he made her? He couldn't, or he wouldn't have been so blithe. Then again, maybe he did. Absolutely livid, Amanda whirled around and marched off toward the street. She knew his eyes were on her; he was smiling as she walked away, but she refused to glance back at him. She slammed into her car and drove off.

By the time she reached the hospital in Parkersville she had cooled down. It was a good thing. Even though it was a short drive, she didn't belong on the road in a pique of temper. No one did.

Both Tommy and Bobby were feeling much better. Amanda lifted the no-visitors ban. "Please call Sheriff Toombs and Mr. Marshall," she told the nurse, "and let them know they can question both boys."

"Mr. Marshall already left a message," the nurse answered. "We'll get him right away."

"Better notify Sheriff Toombs first."

Amanda didn't bother to stick around. She still had her housebound patients to see. For some reason her calls had practically doubled. She didn't discover why until she was halfway through and realized they had all asked the same thing; what were Tyler Marshall's intentions. She had hedged, but by the time she walked into the tenth house, she could almost recite the script. These people weren't ill, they were pretending to be ill so they could interrogate her.

She sighed and went on. All she had left to see was a young child with the measles and an old woman who was lonely and depressed. Surely they would leave her alone.

Amanda turned onto a gravel road. She'd have to hurry if she was going to get to the office on time.

Thankfully there weren't too many cars on the road so she wouldn't be delayed. Actually, there weren't any cars at all on the road. The day was still hot and the humidity lagged in the air. Even so, she found herself relaxing and enjoying the ride. That is, until her car died.

All of a sudden, the old Chevy simply stopped running. She couldn't believe it. She pumped the accelerator pedal and glanced at the gas gauge, which indicated a full tank. The oil pressure was fine, too. She turned the key, hoping. Talk about prophecies. Only the day before yesterday Jimmy John had told her the car was going to break down. What in the world was wrong? She'd just changed the water pump. She pressed down on the accelerator again. Nothing.

Damn! She leaned back in the seat and glanced around at the countryside. The long, hot, dusty road stretched in front of her. Forever. There wasn't a house for miles. No cars. No people. Just trees and plants and an occasional cow, and although this road crossed the one leading into town, Rialto was a long way away.

With a sigh, she got out of the car and lifted the hood, but she may as well have saved her energy. The myriad of wires and hoses coming off the engine were as much a puzzle to her as the human body was to a mechanic. Since she'd put the water pump bolts in yesterday she knew where they went—and that was all.

Disgusted, she closed the hood and dusted off her hands. Now what was she going to do? Jimmy John would be delighted. She could almost hear him cackling with glee: "I told you so, Mandy Lou. I gave ya fair warning." She leaned against the fender and glanced again at her desolate surroundings. In the distance she could see a ball of dust. A car cruising toward her? If only it were someone who could help her. The sheriff, maybe, or a farmer heading into town.

Or Tyler.

If Amanda didn't know better, she would have sworn he'd planned her breakdown, particularly when the ball of dust got closer and she recognized his silver Mercedes. Of all the people to meet on a lonely back road.

As if surprised, Ty slowed when he came near. He pulled up alongside of her and braked to a stop. While she felt disheveled from the heat and dust, he looked cool and collected in the air-conditioned confines of his car. He'd changed from his work clothes into another stylish suit, looking impeccable as usual. "Well," he said, rolling down the window and smiling pleasantly, "it seems we meet again. Something wrong?"

Amanda hated to admit it. "My car's broken down."

"What's the problem?"

"If I knew, I'd fix it," she said testily.

Ty just laughed. "Going somewhere? I'd be glad to give you a lift."

She eyed the sleek, luxurious coupe idling so effortlessly as they spoke. The car represented everything she hated about him. She'd be damned if she got inside. "No, thank you. Aren't you a long way from town? What happened to your house renovations?"

"I got my first call. A farmer out this way wants to talk to me about a tractor warranty. Since I had to go to the hospital to interview Tommy and Bobby, I figured I'd see him, too, on the way back. Sure I can't give you a lift?"

"I have to finish making my rounds."

"I'll take you."

"Won't you be late?"

"Lawyers are always late." His teeth flashed in another good-natured grin. "Or is that what they say about doctors?"

Amanda steamed hotter than the air. "I wouldn't know."

He glanced at her old Chevy. "Did your engine conk out?"

"The car stopped running."

"How about if I take a look at it?" He shut off the Mercedes. "Maybe I can get you going."

Amanda didn't say anything as Ty got out of his car and lifted up the hood of hers. She felt awkward that he had stopped. Now he was helping her.

"How far's your next patient?" he asked.

"Up the road a ways."

"What time do you have office hours?"

"At two."

He glanced at his watch.

"Can you tell what's wrong?" she asked, ashamed of herself. He was being nice, and he could have ignored her, breakdown or no breakdown, and she'd been rotten to him from the moment he'd appeared in town.

He slammed the hood down.

"Can't you fix it?"

"I didn't try. You know, Amanda," he went on after a moment, "it's silly to let your emotions overrule your common sense. I realize you don't want to be near me, but you are stuck. It's a long way back to town and you have patients waiting to see you. Why don't you let me give you a lift?"

She sighed. He was right, of course. But there was

more to her reluctance than just stubbornness. "Ty, if I get in that car with you, people will talk."

"People are already talking. Come on. Get in. I promise not to bite."

Why did he have to sound so sensible? More to the point, why was she letting him get to her? He was acting cool and calm. Then again, he wasn't stuck out here in the country with a broken-down car and a man he didn't want to see. A man who was talking about the past. A man who was touching her. "Wait a minute," she said, pulling away. "I have to get my bag."

The Mercedes was just as luxurious on the inside as on the outside. The upholstery was plush leather, the carpet a better grade than the one she'd had installed in her home. The air-conditioning was so quiet Amanda could barely hear it and yet the air temperature was perfect. A tape played softly in the background as they skimmed over the road with hardly a bump.

"Your car's nice," she said grudgingly after a long moment of silence. "The ride is very smooth."

Ty nodded. "Yes, it is nice."

"I remember you wanted one like it for a long time."

"Mandy, I told you yesterday, I don't intend to apologize for my success."

"I don't expect you to."

"Good. How many patients do you have left to see?"

"Just two. It shouldn't take long."

He shrugged. "Like I said, I don't mind."

She did.

They visited the little girl with measles first. When they pulled up in front of the old farm house, Ty started to get out. "Why don't you just wait for me?" she suggested.

"Do you think that's wise? You pointed out that people will talk. We may as well let everyone see us."

That was true. A few moments later she wondered about his motives as he set about charming both the mother and the little girl. Watching Tyler Marshall in action was an education. Now she could see why she'd been sucked into his trap two years ago, how easy it was to be swayed by his smile and his sincere good-looks.

The little girl had a fever and she'd been crying most of the morning. The mother was at her wits' end, trying to get the child to take aspirin and getting nowhere. While Amanda talked with the mother, Ty produced a coin and started doing magic tricks with it. Pretty soon the child had stopped crying and was watching him make the quarter disappear and reappear behind her ear or in between her toes or up over the lamp. When he was done he convinced her to take the aspirin and some medication for the itching as well, which would relax her and help her sleep.

"Any possibility that you hire out?" the mother asked Ty as they left the room. Exhausted from all her crying, the child had conked out practically the moment she gave in.

"Just for legal advice," he answered. "Got any wills or leases you want drawn up?"

The woman laughed, and headed for a household safe.

Although it only took a moment, Amanda stood dumbfounded as Ty patiently went over the particulars of a warranty deed.

Miss Mabel, the lonely old lady who was the last of her patients, was equally impressed with Tyler. She insisted on fixing lemonade and cookies. "Jimmy John told Miss Gertrude that you have a hankering for home-made lemonade," she said the moment Amanda finished her examination.

And Miss Gertrude had told Mrs. Crowley who had told Miss Mabel. "I'm afraid we won't have time for lemonade," Amanda said. "I've go to get going."

"Nonsense, Mandy Lou." The old lady glanced pointedly at the kitchen clock. "You've got plenty of time. Why, you don't have office hours until two. That's a whole half hour away. It's not every day a famous criminal lawyer comes to visit me. Now relax your body and let me speak to Mr. Marshall for a spell. Tell me, young man, what are you doing in our lovely town?"

"I'm going to take on the Whittiker boy's defense."

Mabel nodded gravely. "The boy is in bad trouble. He needs lots of help."

Ty agreed. "I intend to do everything I can for him."

"That's kind of you. You're a fine lawyer."

Ty smiled at her. "Why, thank you, ma'am. What a nice thing to say."

Amanda almost gagged on his saccharin-sweet tone, but she had a feeling he meant it. He was actually having fun here in Rialto, getting to know the townspeople. By two o'clock she had heard almost all she could bear. "Look, we have to go," Amanda cut in. "I have to be back at the office. I have a lot of patients to see."

"Why, it'd do the towns-folk good to wait on you, Mandy Lou Pearson," Mabel told her. "Everybody takes advantage of you."

Amanda agreed, Mabel included. Letting her patients rule her life was wrong. But her father had always spoiled his patients, too, and so she was accustomed to acclimating her lifestyle to the town. "But it won't help me much to make them wait. I'll be the one falling behind."

"You work too hard. A nice young girl like you should have some time to herself. Might want to go a'courtin' and such. Don't you agree, Mr. Marshall?"

Amanda flushed at the obvious innuendo. "I'm not the courting type, Mabel."

"Isn't that the truth? You've been dating Frank Nelson for nigh onto a year now, and there hasn't been a thing happened between you. Folks are about to give up on you. Now that Mr. Marshall's here—"

Amanda just smiled tolerantly and said, "Excuse me, Mabel, but we really have to be going. Keep taking your vitamins, now," she instructed. "I'll see you tomorrow."

The elderly woman walked them to the door. "Be careful going down," she said when they got to the stairs. "The bottom step is rickety."

"Don't you have anyone to fix it for you?" Ty asked. "It could be dangerous."

"We don't have a carpenter for miles. Why, folks in Rialto do their own work."

"I'll come fix it for you tomorrow," Ty said. "Are you going to be home?"

Mabel beamed. "Would you?"

"I'd be delighted."

When they got in the car Amanda smiled prettily, facetiously. "Gee, Ty, maybe you ought to add 'all around handyman' to the sign in front of your house."

Ty laughed. "Maybe I will." He glanced in the rearview mirror as they pulled away. "She's a pleasant lady."

Amanda nodded. "She's lived a good life."

"Who's Frank?" he asked after a moment.

"The town pharmacist."

"You've been dating?"

"Yes."

"Is he in love with you?"

Did he expect her to just start talking? Act as if nothing were wrong between them? They'd shared one afternoon, but that was because she didn't have a choice. "Look, Ty, I'd rather not discuss it."

"Just curious." The tape played softly and the air-conditioning hummed quietly as they headed back down the road. Ty broke the silence. "You really do care about these people, don't you, Mandy?"

She hadn't really thought about it much. "Yes, I guess I do."

"You wouldn't have done well in Chicago."

She glanced at him. "Is that justification for my not getting the appointment to County Memorial?"

"No. I'm sorry about that. I really am. I know you wanted that appointment. But you're in your element here. These people need you and you need them. And you're right," he went on in a soft, low tone, "I've been trying to ingratiate myself here. I'm sorry. I really like these people, too."

Amanda was shocked at his admission, but she didn't have time to discuss it. In the distance she could see her car. She frowned when Ty pulled up behind the old Chevy. He was supposed to take her to her office. "What are you doing? Where are you going?"

"Thought I'd take another look at your engine," he said, opening his car door and getting out. "It'll just take a minute."

Amanda followed him. "I thought you didn't know what was wrong with it."

He glanced at her. "Did I say that?"

"You said you couldn't fix it."

"I said I didn't try. It's just a condenser coil wire," Ty said, opening the hood and fiddling with a small wire near the housing. "It came off. You probably knocked it loose when you changed the water pump the other day. I'll put it back on and you'll be fine."

Amanda was stunned. "You mean my car wasn't broken?"

"No, it was broken."

"But you knew all along what was wrong with it?"

"Yes," he admitted.

"You lied to me."

"No, I didn't."

"You didn't tell the truth."

"I didn't do that either."

"Dammit, Tyler, you purposely fooled me."

He nodded. "Yes, that's true."

"Just what were you trying to prove?" she asked. "Was this all a ploy to get me to testify, driving me around the countryside, taking me to see my patients?"

"No, Amanda. It was a ploy to be with you." He slammed down the hood of her car and reached through the open window to turn the key. The engine roared to life, sounding as sick as usual. "I'll follow you back to town just to make sure everything is fine," he said. "Better get Jimmy John to do some repair work soon, though. You were lucky this time."

Amanda would have argued with him, but he just walked away and got in his Mercedes. Damn the man.

She jerked her door open so hard it was a wonder it didn't fall off the hinge. Then, slamming inside, Amanda jammed the car in gear and took off down the road, spattering dust and gravel behind her. She knew several stones had hit the Mercedes, but she didn't care. Ty followed her to the block just before her house. At the corner he waved and turned off.

The cars lined up and down her street should have alerted Amanda to the number of people waiting to see her, but she was still simmering about Ty and didn't notice. How could he have tricked her like that, lied to her?

She opened the door to the waiting room and stood still. The place was jammed. Jimmy John Morris flipped through a magazine. Mrs. Crowley had stuffed herself between Miss Gertrude and her husband, and her aunt Sophie was tapping her toe impatiently. It seemed the only people missing in the entire town were her friend, Jean Renee, and the patients she had just seen.

Everyone looked up when she entered. Someone smiled and said, "Afternoon, Doc. You're late."

"What's going on?" Amanda asked. "What are you all doing here?"

Inez answered, her voice light and gay. "Seems as though everyone has developed a virus, Dr. Pearson. I believe it might be termed curiosity—or more appropriately, the Tyler Marshall Syndrome."

Amanda still couldn't believe the number of people in her office. She just stood and shook her head. She'd never seen the townspeople act this way. "This is ridiculous. How many of you are ill?"

They all raised their hands. She glanced at Inez, who

shrugged and said, "I asked the same question. I guess we're bound to see every one of them."

Amanda sighed. The only thing she was bound to do was find a way to get Gordon Tyler Marshall out of her life and out of her town—as soon as possible.

Chapter Five

AMANDA SOON DISCOVERED THAT getting Ty out of her life was going to be a difficult feat, and getting him out of her town was going to be next to impossible. With every passing moment he became more and more entrenched in the hearts and minds of the residents of Rialto. By that afternoon he had achieved sainthood status merely by getting the tractor company to agree to give old Mr. Warren a new tractor to replace the one that had conked out last fall. Amanda heard about that from Jimmy John, who came back to the office just to spread the news. He was going to get Tyler to look at several of his warranties. Maybe Jimmy John could get a new car out of the deal.

When the office emptied at last, Amanda was exhausted again, and that was just from listening to everyone extol the virtues of Gordon Tyler Marshall. She went into the kitchen and brewed a cup of herbal tea.

She needed something to soothe her nerves. One more mention of Ty and she was going to scream.

Half an hour later the doorbell rang. Since she was relaxing, she had changed into a robe and slippers. She had taken off most of her makeup and her hair swirled loose around her shoulders. She'd been reading a medical journal.

"Good evening, Amanda," Ty said when she opened the door. "How are you tonight?"

He stood on her porch, one hand tucked into his pocket, the other holding several papers, looking better than ever. If he was any more attractive he'd need to take out hazard insurance. Even in casual clothes he was sexy, and the dark knit shirt and fashionable slacks he wore only emphasized his lean, tough physique.

"What do you want, Ty?" she asked, irritated. What was it about this man that made her furious with just the slightest provocation? Or in this instance, no provocation at all?

"Still in a bad mood, I see."

"I'm not in a bad mood." Amanda drew the robe tighter around her body in a protective gesture. "I just don't want to be disturbed."

"You mean by me," he amended.

She shrugged. She'd made it clear that she didn't want to see him on a personal basis.

He waved the pages at her. Amanda recognized them as her notes from Tommy Whittiker's hospital chart which he must have had copied. "This isn't a social call. Your writing's getting worse. I can't read what you've recommended. Don't worry," he went on, as though reading her mind. "I went through proper channels and I got permission to have these reproduced so I could talk to you about them."

"I wasn't going to question you."

"Yes, you were."

She shrugged. "What is it you want to know, Ty?"

"Can't I come in?"

"I can read the chart right here."

He glanced around at the darkened night, then at the porch light. Since Rialto was a small town, there weren't any street lamps in the residential sections, and although the moon and stars were bright, they were a dim distance away. "The lighting's not too good. This is important, Amanda. Need I remind you, a boy's life is at stake."

"Fine." Grudgingly she opened the door and let him into her kitchen. "How's Miss Mabel?" she asked as he came inside. "Did you get a chance to fix her stair?"

She knew full well he had; he'd gone back this afternoon and fixed that stair along with several others, and he'd even tightened the screws on her kitchen cabinets. Aunt Sophie had reported that early on.

"Yes. Why? Got anything you want fixed?"

Just my heart, Amanda thought. It was in dire need of repair. "I just wondered." Amanda held out her hand. "May I see the chart?"

"Sure."

She glanced at the papers. "It just says that he's improving. Vital signs normal, lab values normal. Prognosis good."

"That's all?"

"That's it. I know it's disappointing, Ty, but I've told you before, there's nothing unusual about this case. As far as I can see there are no medical surprises, no genetic defects. Tommy is healthy."

"You never know until you look, Amanda."

She nodded. "I agree. But there's nothing here to look at."

Although he took the pages from her, he didn't seem ready to leave. He glanced around the kitchen as though he wanted to sit down. Amanda didn't make the offer. "Would you happen to know where the accident happened?" he asked at last. "I've made inquiries from several people, and no one can seem to pinpoint the place for me."

"You're joking." Every person in town knew where Tommy had run down Bobby. That had been as hot a topic as the crime itself. "It was at the bluff. Lover's Lane."

"I know, but where at the bluff?"

"By the old hickory tree."

"I couldn't find it."

The tree towered over the area. It had to be at least fifty feet tall. "It's awfully hard to miss, Ty."

"If you know trees. I'm a city boy. Can't tell one leaf from another." He paused. "Think maybe you could help me locate the spot, Amanda? I'd like to go over a few things in my mind. I need to get ready for the trial."

"Do you have a trial date already?" She was amazed. In Rialto it took forever just to get a traffic ticket to court, let alone schedule an attempted murder trial.

"Yes, I just heard. We're on the dockets for the end of July. I think Glenn Whittiker must have pulled a few strings."

Undoubtedly since it was only a few weeks away. "Is the trial going to be here?"

"No, Effingham."

That was probably just as well, considering the sympathies in both Rialto and Senton. At least there would be the chance of neutral jurors. "You'll travel back and forth?"

"Probably. Effingham's not that far. Well?" Ty went on. "Think you could help me?"

She may as well be honest with him, even at the risk of sounding egotistical. "This wouldn't be another ploy to be with me, would it?"

He must have adopted a policy of honesty, too. He shrugged. "Maybe. Some. Seriously, Amanda, I would like to see the spot where the incident occurred. I'd like to talk to you, too. Casually, of course. I think we need to clear up some of the animosity between us."

The only thing that would clear that up would be his leaving. "Why now? Why not in the daytime?"

"I fully intend to go back in the daytime. But as I understand it, the incident happened at night. I'd like to see everything the way the kids saw it—as much as I can. It helps me to piece things together, gather details."

Amanda hesitated, not wanting to be near him. Why did he always sound so logical?

He smiled. "Please don't think I'm being devious, but if it will help you make your decision, I should warn you that Mrs. Crowley knows I'm here. She saw me come in. You might want to go just to keep down the gossip. No telling what she thinks we're doing in here."

Although it had nothing to do with convincing her, Amanda had to agree with him. Mrs. Crowley was probably already on the phone spreading rumors. "Wait a minute," Amanda answered. "I'll get dressed."

The night was soft and warm, a typical summer evening in the Midwest. Ty had left the car windows down and a light breeze filtered into the Mercedes, feathering Amanda's hair back from her face. She'd put on slacks and an old sweatshirt, and with her hair pulled back into a ponytail she felt strangely carefree. She leaned back in the seat. A sliver of moon was out and stars studded the sky. For some reason the tiny pinpoints of light seemed brighter out here in the country with no smog or buildings to block the view. Amanda could pick out several constellations.

"The sky is lovely," Ty said.

She nodded. "I'm always amazed at how much you can see out here. When I lived in Chicago I was lucky to find the North star."

He laughed. "Constellations weren't much better in New York, either. I couldn't see over the skyline. Say, is that the infamous pigpen?" he asked as they drove by Mary Cahill's place.

He'd remembered that? Amanda glanced out the window. The pigs were asleep, piled in a corner on top of each other.

"Yes, that's it."

"They look harmless enough."

"They made an absolute mess, though, running up on her porch and knocking over a tree she'd planted. Miss Mary was really upset." Amanda laughed as she remembered the incident. It had been so funny. "And they ate some of her prize corn."

Ty laughed, too. "What's so bad about that? Didn't she want them to get fat?"

"Not on her prize corn. She pickles it and takes it to shows. Poor Tommy, how he smelled!"

"How was his motorcycle?"

"It sank in the mud." She laughed again. "He was so angry. According to Inez, he started swearing and Miss Mary ran into the house with her ears covered."

"That bad?"

"I understand Tommy was quite creative. She'd never heard some of the words. Actually she's never gotten over it. She talks about it to this day. Turn left down here."

The bluff served as the town's lover's lane, probably because it was so private and obscure. The area was crowded by trees and shrubs and underbrush, a direct contrast from the rest of the land, all hilly and rolling down to the river bank. Ty parked the Mercedes near a thick copse of trees, pulling up so that they could see the water, a wide silver ribbon in the darkness of night. Since it was early there weren't any cars parked yet. Around ten o'clock cars would start pulling in. The area was quiet except for the croak of a bullfrog or the splash of a creature downstream.

She gestured off to one side as they got out of the car. "The hickory tree's right over there."

"Well," Ty remarked. "It is hard to miss."

Amanda laughed. "It's kind of a community landmark. Folks say the tree is several hundred years old."

"Does it bear nuts?"

"Oh, yes, all over the place. Even the squirrels can't keep up with the production. Sometimes in the fall the town ladies will gather nuts and do some baking. The rest of the nuts get crushed by all the cars."

Ty examined a nick in the bark of the tree. Hickory wood was hard, but Tommy had run his motorcycle into it, and there was a fresh scar. "I understand Sandy told

Tommy she was pregnant that night," he said. "I wonder why they came here?"

"I think they wanted privacy. There aren't any teen clubs in town and there are few places for kids to go. I heard it was around this time at night. There wasn't anyone here yet."

"Too bad. It would have been nice to have a witness." Ty glanced around the area. "It's quiet."

"Very."

He knelt and sifted the leaves under the tree. "Everything seems so normal. I wish I knew what happened."

"Didn't the sheriff take pictures?" Amanda asked. "Go over the area for evidence?"

"Yes." Ty stood up. "He's given me what they have, but there was very little to find, except for tire tracks and nicks in the tree."

"What about Tommy?"

"He doesn't remember anything." As Amanda recalled he'd been mute from the start. "Frankly, I don't think he wants to remember anything."

"Sandy?"

"She was crying. She says she didn't see much until the accident was over. All she could tell me was that the boys were fighting, but everyone already knows that. Tommy was leaving. He was getting on his motorcycle. Sandy looked up and he ran into Bobby, pinning him to the tree."

It seemed cut and dry, and yet so very vague. "That's all you have?"

"So far."

"What are you going to do?"

"I don't know. I'll think of something." He sighed

and took her hand. "Come on, let's go down by the river."

It didn't occur to Amanda to object. It just seemed natural to walk beside him to the banks of the river. They were at the scene of a crime, after all, and looking for evidence. But her hand tingled from his touch and her body shivered from his nearness.

They stood looking at the water. "I wonder what it was like for the settlers that came here," he said all of a sudden. "I wonder what they thought when they saw the river. How the land was built up, the city."

What an odd subject. Amanda never knew Ty to be interested in history. "I imagine they thought it a good place to settle," she said. "Rialto means marketplace."

"Do you think they envisioned a great city on the banks of a river?"

Amanda shrugged. "I don't know. It's an old town, but I never delved much into the history, and it's built back from the river."

"Maybe that was smart, considering how some rivers flood," he remarked.

"Maybe," Amanda agreed. "The river is still important, though, if only as a source of recreation. We fish a lot around here. I do know that the people who live here have descended from long generations."

"Was your father from Rialto?" Ty asked curiously.

"No. My mother lived here. My father was hired to be the town doctor. She was his first patient."

"What was wrong with her?"

Amanda smiled, remembering the story. "Just a sore throat. Unfortunately, or fortunately, however you view it, my father was a very progressive physician, and he traipsed right into my mother's bedroom unescorted, and examined her, not realizing what her parents might think. Everyone was horrified. My father always joked that he had two choices, die or propose on the spot. He decided to propose."

Ty laughed. "And they lived happily ever after?"

"Yes." Amanda nodded. "Very happily. Sometimes I think life was simpler back then."

"You may be right. Certainly the choices were simpler." Silence stretched between them. All of a sudden he asked huskily. "Do you still like spaghetti?"

So he remembered their dinner, too. Amanda would never forget it. She glanced at him. The moonlight played on his features much as it had on the river, making his face all silvery, reflecting off his dark hair. God, how she'd loved him, still loved him. They were standing close together, the sounds of the night in the background, the softness of the summer evening.

Too close. Too soft.

Ty slowly lowered his head to hers. He was going to kiss her. Quickly she turned away. "No. I don't like spaghetti."

"Amanda," he called as she pulled from his grasp and started up the river bank. She had to get away. She had to keep him at arm's length. One touch and she would be gone. But he caught her by the hand. "What's the matter, Amanda? Please tell me what's wrong."

How could he ask that? Didn't he know? "I don't think we should discuss the past, Ty." Why had she been standing there talking with him at all, letting him hold her hand? "I really think we should keep our relationship on an impersonal basis. I told you that the day you came here."

"Amanda, wait," he said when she pulled away

again. "Look, I'm sorry. We won't talk about the past. Okay?"

She still didn't trust him. Or herself. "We should go home, Ty. It's getting late."

"Amanda," he said, his voice torn, "how can I convince you that my convictions are honorable? What do you want from me? What can I do?"

She shook her head. Even though two years had passed, her wounds were still too raw. "You can't convince me, Ty. It's impossible. You could tell it to the world and I wouldn't believe it."

"Would you at least listen?"

She sighed. She hated splitting hairs with him. "It's the same thing. Look, Ty, I don't want to argue with you, and I'm really tired of telling you I want to keep things on a professional basis. Could you please take me home?"

He hesitated a moment. Then he shrugged and started up the bank. "Sure. Come on."

When Ty dropped her off Amanda was certain it was the last she would see of him. At her door he glanced down at her almost sadly and traced his finger along her lips as he murmured, "I won't bother you again."

Surprisingly, watching him walk away, she felt somewhat let down at how easily he had accepted her rebuke. She had expected a fight.

No, she finally admitted the following morning, she had *wanted* a fight. Inez was her usual cheerful self, bringing in the mail along with tales from town. "I hear you had a good time last night."

"Excuse me?" Amanda glanced up from the X-ray report she was reading.

"You were with GTM. Didn't you expect it to get back?"

"Who is GTM?" It sounded like a car.

"Who else? Gordon Tyler Marshall. Interested in what's being said?"

Amanda couldn't help sighing. She hated herself for her soulful laments, and for her curiosity. "I can hardly contain myself."

When Inez was finished relating the story Amanda sighed again. Amazing, she hadn't seen a single person at the bluff, and yet everyone in town knew that she and Ty had stood on the riverbank for exactly twenty-two minutes and six-point-five seconds and that they had discussed the town heritage and that Ty had taken her hand to help her down the riverbank. That is, after they had examined the crime site and he had spent ten minutes inside her house. Alone with her.

Amanda just shook her head. "How many patients do we have to see today?"

"Slightly less than half the population." Inez smiled. "If we hurry, we might get done early."

"How's Ted?"

"Still dying."

Amanda laughed. "Men."

"You can say that again," Inez reiterated.

Ty was true to his word. He didn't bother Amanda again, not even with medical questions. She didn't see him for several days, but she didn't have to see him to know his every move. Every breath he took was reported to her in onerous detail by at least ten people. One by one he seemed to be charming the townsfolk. It got to the point where she hated listening to them extol his virtues. Either he was off fixing someone's house or he was going over their contracts or he was working hard to save "poor" Tommy Whittiker. (She didn't bother to remind them that just a few days ago "poor" Tommy Whittiker had been a black sheep in this town.)

In his leisure time Ty sat with the men over in front of the grocery store, gossiping and sipping lemonade. Someone told her he'd even taken up whittling and was carving himself a statue of justice. Amanda found herself feeling jealous. The man fit into the town as though he'd been born to it. Even Jean Renee had started singing his praises.

"Have you seen what he's done with that old Miller house?" her friend called to ask. It was night, and Amanda didn't have much to do. She'd kept the phone off the answering machine. "Mandy, it's gorgeous."

"I don't want to talk about Tyler," Amanda answered. "Isn't there any other news in town?"

"Not that's interesting to report. The scandal's all died down: Tommy's been given bond, Bobby's recuperating, Sandy's getting bigger by the day. Looks like Tyler's got everything under control. We just have to wait for the trial. Say, are you going to the Fourth of July bash tomorrow?"

"I wish I could get out of it." Not only would the town be upset if she skipped the annual picnic, Frank was expecting her.

She still hadn't decided what to do about him. He'd called her and they'd gone out to dinner. They hadn't talked about their relationship, though. When she'd brought up the subject, asking if he'd heard the rumors about her and Ty, he'd asked, "You're not seeing Tyler anymore, are you?"

"Well, no," she answered.

"Then don't worry about it. I like to spend my time with you, and I'm willing to take my chances." Amanda really didn't think he cared for her. He seemed as enamored of her as she was of him, but he just didn't know it. Tyler's presence had threatened him.

"Oh, Mandy, it's fun," Jean went on, talking about the town festival. "You're getting to be such a spoilsport these days. You don't want to go anywhere."

"Look, Jean, you don't have to fix a lunch and stand up on a stage and be auctioned off like someone's prize cow." As one of the single women in town, Amanda was expected to participate in the charity box luncheon. The only good thing about it was that the proceeds went to the Little League baseball team.

"No, but just think, I get to participate in the quilting contest."

Amanda laughed. "True." Jean Renee couldn't sew a stitch.

"I wish they would make a division for the most kids," her friend went on. "I'd win hands down."

Something warned Amanda to ask, an inflection in her voice, "Are you pregnant again, Jean?" After the last child, when Jean had been so sick, she'd warned her friend that a bit of birth control was in order.

"Amanda—"

"Oh, Jean."

"I can't help it. Dan and I are in love."

Amanda sighed. "There are lots of ways to express your love, Jan."

"But none that are as great as sex." Her voice softened, melted. "And you know how I love babies. I'm working on an even dozen."

Amanda shook her head in amazement. How could any one woman in this day and age love children so much that she would have twelve? But love them Jean did, and she was a wonderful mother. "Look, you better come in so I can give you a good examination, and I'm going to insist that you go on a strict diet."

"I promise, I won't cheat. Oh, Mandy, I'm so excited."

"So am I, Jean," Amanda admitted. "I'm just naturally cautious."

"Not really, Mandy. Inside you're as soft-hearted as I am. You just don't show it." She paused. "Have you seen Tyler lately?"

So they were back to that. "No."

"Are you going to?"

"Not if I can help it."

"Don't be so hard on him, Mandy. He loves you."

"Oh, please."

"What does he have to do to prove to you that he's sincere? The man is—"

Amanda was growing exasperated. "The man has been in town for a little more than a week," she cut in, "and everyone thinks I should drop at his feet. What do I have to do to convince you that all Ty wants is fame and fortune?"

"I haven't seen it, Mandy. He doesn't act the way you say he is, and for some reason he just doesn't strike me as the type to use people."

That was something Amanda had to agree on. Why was it that Ty seemed so sincere? It was an act. It had to be. He'd hurt her. But she wasn't sure anymore. "You know, Jean, sometimes I don't think he realizes that he is using people. I think he thinks it's all right. I know he thinks that what he's doing is right."

Jean Renee sighed. "You never did go into much detail about what broke you up, but if he believed what you did was right, maybe it was right. He's the lawyer."

"I don't know." Amanda supposed it all came down to how she felt, and whether or not she had been right or wrong, she *felt* as though she'd been wrong. "I guess I just don't want to take the chance. You know he lied to me the other day when my car broke down."

"Oh, come on, Amanda, are you really going to hold that against him?"

"Jean, a lie is a lie."

"Not really. The man wanted to see you. I'd be flattered if someone went to that extreme just to be with me."

"The next time my car's broken down, I'll give you a call."

Jean laughed. "Just don't burn your bridges, Mandy. Give the guy a chance."

"I don't want to be hurt."

"I know," Jean answered, "but don't forget, bitterness makes a lonely companion." In the background a child started crying. "Hey, I gotta go."

"Sure," Amanda said. "Talk to you later. Make an appointment," she added, but the line was broken.

After she hung up, Amanda stood staring at the phone for several long moments. Was she just feeding her bitterness? She wished she knew. She also wished she knew why Ty had come here to small-town America—the real reason. But that was another missing answer. If he did care for her why hadn't he tried to see her for the past few days? Perhaps it was because she'd told him to stay away?

Not wanting to think about it any longer, she went into the kitchen to make a lunch for the celebration tomorrow. Tyler Marshall was a puzzle she might never figure out, and at the moment she wasn't going to try.

And as for tomorrow, maybe it would rain.

Chapter Six

THE FOURTH OF JULY dawned beautifully. There wasn't a cloud in the sky. The morning sun rose up over the horizon all bright and orange and disgustingly warm, with the promise of a lovely day. Amanda puttered around for several hours, wasting time. She didn't have any patients to see, except Bobby, and he was doing fine. The hospital had called to tell her he was sleeping, and not to hurry in. She could even skip the day if she wanted to. Seemingly no one needed her. Even the little girl who had the measles was up on her feet and coming to the town celebration, as was Miss Mabel.

Everyone would be there. Amanda was certain Tyler had been invited, particularly the way the town had embraced him. She wouldn't be surprised if they made him the honored guest. They could cart him through the festivities on a litter, all bowing down and paying homage to him.

Amanda shook her head, disgusted with herself. Why was she being so nasty? Ty hadn't done anything to make her so vehement. It wasn't his fault that the townspeople adored him. She just wished they wouldn't make it so obvious, and that they didn't expect her to adore him, too.

She opened the refrigerator and pulled out the box lunch she'd made last night. Because she'd been angry she'd thrown together a peanut butter sandwich, figuring whoever bought her lunch deserved what they got. It was wrapped up in a pretty package, tied with a pink ribbon. She thought about making something good, but she changed her mind when she remembered that she had to stand up on a stage and the town widowers would bid for her presence for the day. It was archaic and chauvinistic and everything else she could think of but fun. Frank would win. He'd already told her he was bidding.

But Ty might bid also, which was the real reason she'd made peanut butter.

Figuring she'd better show up before someone called to check on her, she pulled a sweater out of the closet and tossed it around her shoulders. The day always ended with a fireworks display and it could get chilly. The thin silk blouse and slacks she wore wouldn't keep her very warm. She picked up the box lunch and went out the door.

The town celebration was held in the same place every year, a park right in the middle of town. In addition to a livestock showing by the men, and crafts and cooking demonstrations by the women, a carnival had been brought in to entertain the children and teens. Even at ten in the morning everything was in full swing—

rides were going, barkers were calling, games were being played. A fortune teller read a crystal ball and someone else guessed weights and ages.

Jean Renee and Daniel had brought all the kids. Amanda didn't need a pregnancy test to confirm that her friend was pregnant. One look and she knew—Jean practically glowed. Daniel also seemed pretty proud. They sat with Amanda under a tent sipping a soda.

"We're going to have to put on another room," Daniel said, watching as one of the boys scurried by, headed for the Ferris wheel.

"Why don't you just make your current rooms into a dorm?" Amanda teased. "That way you won't have to worry about who's going to share."

"It's the bathroom I'm worried about," Jean Renee spoke up. "We have five girls already. Wait until they get to be teenagers, and get ready for dates."

Amanda laughed as Daniel's mouth fell open, as though just realizing how they would monopolize the room. "That's it, Jean," he said, "we're stopping at nine."

"Aw, honey," she pouted, "I love kids."

Amanda shook her head. "Wait until you have to start sewing wedding dresses."

Jean sat up straight. "I hate to sew."

"You better start liking it."

"Ugh." She stuck out her tongue. "Speaking of wedding dresses," she said, her expression brightening, "where's Frank?"

Amanda stuck out her tongue back. "Revenge doesn't become you."

Jean laughed. "Well you won't talk about Ty." She glanced around. "I wonder where he is?"

"Maybe we'll get lucky and he won't come."

"Ouch!" Daniel flinched. "Strong words. I gather you're still angry at him."

Amanda shrugged.

"I'm sure he'll be here. I hear he's bringing Miss Mabel."

But by lunch time he still hadn't shown up. Amanda pretended she didn't notice, but she couldn't help wondering about him. Was this some game he was playing, piquing her interest by playing hard to get? If so, it was working. Frank had appeared and they sat around doing nothing for several long minutes. She was almost glad when the auction started. It was the highlight of the day. One by one the lunches were bid on and couples paired off, most of them young lovers. Everyone laughed and poked fun. Amanda sat in the audience and watched, dreading her turn.

"By the way, I'll bid on your lunch," Frank whispered when the auctioneer was halfway through the packages, "but I hope you don't mind if I don't eat it."

She frowned at him. "Why?"

"I'm trying to lose some weight."

The man was rail thin. "You look fine, Frank."

"I don't look like Tyler Marshall."

"Oh." Not many people did. Amanda didn't bother to tell Frank it would take more than a diet to accomplish that feat.

"Do you mind? I'll take the food home and save it."

She felt guilty. "You know, Frank, maybe you shouldn't bid on my lunch."

"Why?"

"It's not very good and—" She didn't know how else

to put it. She sighed. "We don't exactly have a burning relationship, Frank."

"I don't mind." He smiled at her. "Passion isn't important to me, Amanda."

How odd. "What is important to you?" Amanda wasn't just asking. She really wanted to know. She was tired of vacillating, of feeling guilty, seeing someone she didn't care for, of being thrown together.

"Companionship. Warmth. You're a lovely person, Mandy."

"Thank you. That's nice of you to say." The auctioneer was almost to her package, but she was still confused, concerned. "Are you sure you don't want more than companionship, Frank? Don't you want to be in love?"

"Wish not, want not. Love is for kids, Amanda. We're adults."

She sighed again. She wished she could be as content with nothing. The auctioneer had picked up her lunch. "Excuse me. I'll be right back."

"I'll bid."

She smiled. "Fine."

This was the part she hated. She forced herself to walk forward.

"Well, well, well," the auctioneer said when she arrived on stage beside him. "Mandy Lou's lunch. What'd you fix, Mandy Lou?" he asked her, weighing the package in his hand. "Why, it's light as a feather. You must be improvin' as a cook."

"Must be," she joked back. She stood holding her hands in front of her demurely, her sweater tossed over her shoulders.

"Look at her, fellas," he addressed the audience,

"even if she can't cook, she's a mighty fine doc, and according to the rules, you get to spend the day with her. All day. Just think, if you get hurt, she can fix you right up." A twitter of laughter rose from the watching crowd. "Let's see, what'll we start with? How about five dollars for Mandy Lou's light lunch?"

Frank held up his hand. "Five."

"Do I hear seven dollars?"

"Seven dollars," somebody said.

"Ten," Frank countered.

If things went the way they had for the past two years, Amanda knew they'd stop at fifteen and let Frank eat lunch with her. But she hadn't counted on Ty.

Or had she?

All of a sudden he spoke up from the edge of the crowd, his low, sexy voice curling through the air. "Excuse me, Nate. Does lemonade happen to come with the lunch?"

The auctioneer glanced at him. "Why, Tyler, I was wondering where you were."

He smiled, that million-dollar grin. He was wearing slacks and another casual polo shirt that emphasized his physique, and his dark hair glistened in the sunlight. He had cocked his sunglasses on top of his head. "I was delayed getting here. Miss Mabel had a list of chores for me to do."

"Got to watch the women, Tyler. They'll work you to death." The auctioneer glanced at Amanda. "Does lemonade come with your lunch, Mandy Lou?"

She glared at Ty. How dare he come here and embarrass her this way. He was supposed to leave her alone. "No, it doesn't."

"She says no. Will you bid anyhow?"

Ty shrugged. "Why not? One hundred dollars."

"One hundred dollars!" the auctioneer sputtered. "Well, for a lunch without lemonade that's pretty good. What do you say, Frank?"

The pharmacist turned red. "That's a little steep, isn't it?"

"Depends on how bad you want to be with her," the auctioneer answered, which drew another round of laughter from the crowd.

"One hundred one," Frank said.

Things were getting out of hand. Amanda stepped forward, about to break up the foolishness when Ty called out, "Five hundred."

A gasp went up from the crowd. "Five hundred dollars!" the auctioneer repeated.

"One thousand," Ty said quietly.

Someone choked.

"Tyler, you don't have to bid higher," the auctioneer paused and said, "nobody bid against you."

"It's for charity, right?" Ty asked.

"Yes, sir."

"Then I bid one thousand."

"One thousand." The auctioneer puffed his chest out and grinned. "One thousand," he said again as though he couldn't get over it. "You must want to be with her bad."

"Just get it over with, will you?" Amanda hissed from behind the man.

"Are you upset, Mandy Lou? Why, I believe you're upset. One thousand going once—"

"Please," she said, watching Frank get up and leave the audience. This was all her fault.

"Sold!" the auctioneer proclaimed. "To Mr. Tyler Marshall for one thousand dollars."

Amanda must have been throwing off sparks. When she stepped down off the stage no one came near her. Except Ty. He came up to her as blithely as you please, and took the lunch from her hands.

Still trying for laughter, the auctioneer called out, "Hey, Tyler, for that kind of money, I think I'd ask for a little kiss, too."

Ty just smiled and nodded. "Will do."

Amanda could hardly contain her fury. "I thought you weren't going to bother me anymore," she said.

"I changed my mind." He glanced at her, taking in her flashing eyes and clenched jaw. "Are you angry?"

"That's putting it mildly."

He shrugged. "Well, it's certainly nothing new, particularly where I'm concerned. You know, Amanda, I'm not really such a bad guy."

"No," she agreed, her voice silky sweet, "you're not a bad guy at all. You've just bought new uniforms for the entire Little League baseball team and you've managed to make a fool of me in front of the whole town in the process."

Ty stood holding her lunch. "No one can make a fool of you unless you let them."

"Oh, please, Ty." Angrily she waved his explanation away. "How like you to blame it on me."

"I'm not going to argue with you, Amanda. Just so you know, everyone is watching. You can either go off in a huff or make the best of the situation."

His warning made her glance around at everyone. Jean Renee and Daniel stood inside the tent next to Jimmy John. Miss Gertrude and Miss Mabel sat nearby.

Her Aunt Sophie was already bent over, whispering to Mrs. Crowley. Even the auctioneer had stopped selling lunches because the crowd had turned toward Ty and Amanda.

"You know, Tyler Marshall," she said, glancing back at him. "I've finally figured out what it is about you that makes me so angry. It's your arrogance."

"All I did was help a charity event."

She noticed Frank pulling from the parking lot in his car. It was too late to do anything about him. "You've hurt a fine man."

Ty followed her gaze. "I didn't do anything to him, Amanda."

But she had; she'd hurt Frank by leading him on for the past two years. She knew that now. She should have broken it off. Actually she shouldn't have let it happen in the first place. Whether or not Frank cared for her, she had given him false hopes.

"Did you want to eat lunch with him?"

She glanced back at Ty. "No, but I don't want to eat lunch with you, either."

"Fine." He placed the box down on a table and took her arm, steering her away from the crowds. "Let's go for a walk. We'll eat later."

She pulled away. "I think you missed the point, Ty. I don't want to be with you, period."

He paused when she did. "I didn't miss the point. I just avoided it, like you do."

"What do you mean by that?"

"Amanda, if you didn't want to participate in this, why did you make a lunch?" he asked. When she glared at him without an answer, he went on, "You know, you let these people treat you like a child, and then you complain when they do."

"What is this, pick on Amanda day?" She was furious at the way he was attacking her.

"No, it's face the truth day." He stood glaring down at her. From the look on his face he was growing as frustrated as her. "You hide behind these people and then you blame them for the situation you're in."

"How do you know what I do?" She was growing more and more furious. "You don't know these people, Ty. This is my town. I don't want to hurt anyone."

"You can't hurt people by standing up to them. You hurt them by not being honest."

Amanda was growing weary of his accusations. Unfortunately his words had a ring of truth. "Look," she snapped, "did you want to have lunch with me or not?"

"Yes."

"Then let's go." She snatched the box from the table and started walking away.

She was halfway across the fairgrounds when Ty caught her arm. "I'm sorry, Amanda," he said softly, pulling her around to face him. "You're right. It's none of my business. This is your town, and these are your people."

She sighed, his apology taking the thunder from her fury. Why did they have to argue so much? "I wish I didn't have to admit this, but you have a point, Ty," she answered. "When I came back home I fell into the old trap."

"It's not bad."

"But it's not good. I know that."

"You're a good doctor, Amanda, and you're a good resident of Rialto."

She laughed, amused by his attempt to compliment her. Most men would tell her she was beautiful or vivacious or a good conversationalist. Only Ty would think she was a good citizen. "Thanks."

"It's good to see you laugh, Mandy."

"It's good *to* laugh. We're being silly, aren't we?"

He nodded. "And we're adults too. Think we can get along for the day? After all, I did buy your lunch, and accordingly to the rules, we stay together until I eat it."

"Sure." She was weary of fighting. "I'm sorry about Frank."

"So am I." Odd, they'd formed a truce of sorts. Perhaps that was what was needed, though, to get through the day and all the days to come. Amanda glanced around. Everyone was still watching them. She'd get lots of phone calls tonight. "Where do you want to go?"

"It's hot. I'd like to find some lemonade."

She smiled again. The man had to have a fettish for the stuff. "I know just the place."

The café on Main Street was almost ready to close. Most of the Rialto was at the celebration. But the waitress was glad to pour them a glass of lemonade to go.

"Mmm," Ty said, taking a sip as they strolled back down the street. "Marvelous."

It was fresh-squeezed, ice-cold and sweet, just slightly tart, a country tradition, and it did taste good. Amanda sipped hers slowly.

"How's your car?" Ty asked when they passed an old beater parked along the street.

"Fine. I haven't had any more breakdowns."

"Did you get it checked out?"

"Yes. Jimmy John took a look at it. There's not much he can do, unfortunately. He has a theory about cars, he says they're like women, necessary but recalcitrant."

"He told you that?" Ty grinned, obviously amused. "Can you imagine him saying something like that in Chicago? The feminists would choke him to death."

"I've given it great consideration myself."

"He's a nice guy," Ty said.

"Do you really think I let them walk all over me?" Amanda asked quietly. The subject brought his accusation back.

"Yes. You need to stand up for yourself, Amanda. You have free will."

Then what was she doing here with him?

The question of the decade. That was something she didn't want to think through. She wasn't sure she would like the answer. They passed the carnival midway going back. Amanda was hoping they might run into Jean Renee and Daniel. If she had to be with Ty, it would be better for her if they weren't alone. Just his presence sent shivers of awareness up her spine.

But she didn't have to worry about it. Given the behavior of the residents of Rialto, she couldn't have been alone with him even if she'd tried. They had barely crossed the street when Jimmy John came rushing forward. "Tyler, Mandy Lou, if you don't hurry you're going to miss the bingo game."

"Bingo?" Ty repeated.

"Ain't you ever played bingo?" Jimmy John looked horrified. "Why it's a town tradition, 'specially at the Fourth of July festival."

"I see."

Amanda could tell Ty was thrilled. She smiled facetiously, her eyes teasing him. "What was that you were telling me about free will?"

He glanced at her. "You really want to play bingo?"

"Of course." He knew she didn't. "What fun."

He laughed and took her hand. "You're going to regret that choice, Mandy Lou Pearson. Come on, let's hit the jackpot."

Actually bingo wasn't so bad. Ty made it fun. He kept getting confused and arguing about the numbers and buying more cards. Finally the caller declared everyone a winner and gave out prizes just to clear the tent. But right after that they had to participate in the sack races and then Mrs. Crowley insisted they try the cake walk. Ty might want to select the blackberry cake she had baked. Of course, she didn't tell him he had to buy tickets. Once he found out, he bought the whole roll.

Amanda had forgotten how charming he could be, and how much fun she had with him. By the end of the day he still hadn't eaten her lunch. He sat on the ground and pulled her down beside him. Most everyone else had paired off for dinner. People sat on blankets interspersed around the lawn.

"It's getting late," she said, anxious for him to see what he'd paid so much money for, "aren't you hungry?"

"I'm starved."

"Them why don't you eat?"

He held the box in his hand. "I can't help being suspicious, Amanda. What'd you put in here?"

"Nothing," she said innocently. "How was I to know you were going to bid?"

He studied her for a long moment. "We've had fun, haven't we?" he said softly, tracing his finger along her lips like he had that night they'd gone to the bluff. "It's been a nice day."

"Yes," she agreed, shivering from the warmth of his touch, "it's been a wonderful day."

"But?"

Why did there have to be a but? He read her well. She'd been dreading this moment. She drew a deep breath and glanced away. "I can't forget, Ty. I wish I could."

"What happened in Chicago?"

"Yes."

All around her people talked and laughed, children giggled, music played, insects chirped, and yet the silence grew deep, telling. "Isn't there anything I can do to beg your forgiveness, Amanda? How long are you going to punish me?"

She was surprised at his assumption, at the agony in his tone. She glanced back at him. "You think I'm punishing you?"

"What else do you call it? Every time I get near you, you turn away. Every time I try to explain what happened, you refuse to listen."

She had to protect herself, didn't she? She had to steel her emotions. "Ty, I can't let you into my life," she said, picking some clover and weaving the vines together. "I'm sorry if you can't understand that, but it's the way it has to be."

"Because of the people here?"

"No, because you deceived me, and whether you want to believe it or not, it hurt."

Another long silence stretched between them. Finally he said softly, "You know, Amanda, somebody once said: if you trust too much you can be deceived, but if you trust too little, you'll live in torment. I wonder if your deception isn't your torment?"

"You deceived me, Ty."

"I keep trying to prove to you that I don't have any ulterior motives. Nor did I have any, ever—even in Chicago. My only sin was falling in love with you. I've come here and bared my soul. What more do you want from me?"

She wanted what he couldn't give her. Assurances that she wouldn't get hurt. She looked away again, unthreading the clover. The sun was a low, orange ball on the horizon. It would be dark soon. To the west, dark clouds had gathered. Sometime during the night it would storm. "Maybe you better eat your lunch, Ty?"

"You're so stubborn, Amanda."

She shrugged, tossing the weeds aside. "You already know that."

"I suppose I do. Want part of my lunch?" he asked a few moments later. "Even though I hate for the day to end, I guess I'd better eat it."

She turned back to him. He was lying there on the ground, so very earnest. The breeze had ruffled his dark hair, a lock fell appealingly over his forehead. "Is that why you haven't opened it?"

"Yes."

"You're going to be disappointed."

"Why?"

"It's a peanut butter sandwich."

He gave a half-laugh. "Did you make it for Frank?"

"No," she said, "I made it for you."

"How did you know I would bid?"

"I didn't." Dare she? Yet she had to say it. "I just hoped you would."

"Amanda, would you please listen to me?"

She licked her lips nervously. Didn't she owe it to herself to hear him out? Just once, to know the truth? "Can you take me home, Ty? If we're going to talk, I'd like for it to be in private."

He glanced around at all the people. Then he stood and helped her up. "Sure. Come on, let's go."

She paused. "There's going to be a fireworks display later."

"Did you want to see it?"

"Not really. But no one leaves before it."

"Can we watch it from the house?"

He had missed the point. "Yes, I suppose we could."

They rode home in silence. Since everyone was at the festival the town seemed empty—eerie. There were no lights shining, no one sitting on their porch, studying the night. "I'll make some tea," Amanda said when they parked and went inside her house.

"You're not trying to put things off, are you? We're still going to talk?"

"Yes," she answered, "but I always talk over tea."

"Okay." He smiled. "Tea it is, then."

Amanda didn't have any calls on her recorder so she took the phone off the answering machine. It rang almost the moment she walked away.

"What me to get it?" Ty asked.

"If you don't mind. I'll go ahead and put on the teapot. Just take a message, unless it's an emergency."

She had barely set the water on to boil when Ty held up the phone. "It's Frank on the line," he said in a low, quiet tone. "He wants to know your intentions. Seems to be the question of the day."

"Why? What do you mean?"

"I'd like to know your intentions, too."

Deliberately Amanda looked away, taking the phone. "I'm sorry, Frank," she said, twisting the cord as she spoke. "Yes, I know you were embarrassed. Yes, Tyler's here. Yes, I know there will be talk. I'm very sorry."

She hung up the phone and stood for a moment. Then she walked across the room.

"Where are you going?" Ty asked.

"To turn out the lights." She flicked off the lamp and said, "I think it's time this town discovered that I'm all grown up. Ty?" she murmured, "will you stay with me?"

"Just like that?"

"Yes."

Why didn't he answer? She could feel his presence, like heat lightning on a hot summer night. Very slowly he moved beside her, close, so close that she could feel the heat of his body, but instead of kissing her, he reached behind her and flicked the lights back on. "I want you to take note of my morals in this situation, Dr. Amanda Louise Pearson," he said in a low, husky tone. "I'm not going to be a party to compromising your name."

"I thought you said I needed to stand up to the town."

"You do, but if we spend the night together, it's going to be because you want to be with me, and not to show your independence from the town."

"Ty?"

He had started for the door. He paused, glancing back at her. "Yes?"

"Are you leaving?"

"I think it's best if I do. Don't you?"

"Probably," she agreed. "Just so you know, it was never your morals I questioned. It was your ethics."

"They go hand in hand."

"I don't want to be hurt again, Ty."

"Neither do I, Amanda."

Chapter Seven

THE TEA KETTLE WHISTLING made Amanda turn from the door to the stove. She'd been standing in the middle of the room, staring after Ty. It had surprised her that he'd left, and disappointed her as well. Yet, had she expected him to just tumble in bed with her? Or was that in fact what she'd really wanted? She'd learned a lot about herself during the past few days, the most distressing of which was her penchant for avoiding things that she didn't want to face. Had this been just another way to hide from the truth? Had she suspected he would leave, invited it?

Had she chased him away?

She turned off the flame and leaned against the counter, still thinking. Not only was she prone to ignoring the facts, she was unfair. She'd accused Ty of so many things, none of which she had been able to prove. The entire time he'd been in Rialto he'd behaved in an exemplary manner, personally as well as professionally. *She* was the one who had vacillated and acted ridiculously. She wasn't even certain any more if the things she'd accused him of were valid. The entire time they'd been in Chicago he'd also demonstrated high moral and ethical standards—with that one exception. Was it possible that she'd been wrong about him? And about the incident?

So, now that she had reached that conclusion, now what? It seemed that she had two choices: either go to bed or go to Ty and listen to his side of the story. Both would be difficult to do. Amanda pushed from the counter and went to look out the window. The petunias that she had planted were growing, blooming profusely, hot pink against the red brick. A few weeds peeked their ugly heads through. She should pull them.

She was procrastinating again.

Tossing her sweater over her shoulders, she placed the phone back on the answering machine, picked up her beeper and went out the door before she could change her mind.

The town celebration was still in full swing. Amanda could hear the festivities as she hurried to her car. It wasn't quite late enough for the fireworks display yet, dusk was just falling. Lightning bugs were starting to flicker here and there and an occasional cricket chirped, calling to its mate. Soon there would be a cacophony of calls, typical evening sounds in the country, the trill of a mockingbird, the croak of a frog. Few people were out on the streets.

Amanda drove to Ty's and pulled in the driveway. Most of his house was darkened; a single light glowed from his living room window. She'd yet to see the improvements he'd made in the old Miller home, but she did notice the sign out front, swinging gently from the porch column, and she had to smile. It was carved from wood and read: GORDON TYLER MARSHALL, ATTORNEY AT LAW AND ALL AROUND HANDYMAN. Odd, it looked as if it belonged on the old white frame home.

She went up the steps and knocked, lightly at first, and then louder when he didn't answer. She was about to give up when the door opened and he stood in the entrance.

"Amanda?" Clearly Ty was surprised to see her. He had relaxed. His shoes were off and he was wandering around barefoot. His hair was mussed, as though he'd been running his hand through it or lying on the sofa.

"Hi," she said, talking through the screen.

"Is something wrong?"

She could hardly just blurt it out. *No matter what happened between us I'm in love with you. I'll always love you.* Her palms were sweating and she wiped her hands on her pants. *Please help me, Ty.* "I guess that depends on your point of view. You didn't collect your kiss."

He frowned. "My what?"

He wasn't going to make it any easier. "You paid a thousand dollars for my lunch today," she explained, hoping she'd made the right decision, praying. "You never did eat it."

"Are you offering it to me again?"

"No." She smiled nervously. "I don't even have it."

"I don't understand, Amanda."

She took a deep breath. "I thought you were supposed to get a kiss, too. Or at least I thought you were supposed to ask for one."

"You came all the way over here to tell me that?"

"This is a small town, Ty. It's not that far."

He paused a moment. "No," he said in a low, quiet tone, "but we're not talking distance, are we?"

"No."

"What are we talking about?"

She had to say it. "Apologies. Forgiveness, maybe. Understanding."

"From who?"

"Both of us." It was odd talking to him through the screen door. Because of the way the light behind him shadowed his face, all she could see was the outline of his features and the stark white of his shirt. She couldn't tell what he was thinking, feeling. "I'm sorry, Ty. I think I've misjudged you. I'm ready to listen if you're willing to talk."

"I've always been willing to talk."

"I know. I've been stubborn. I'm sorry." She waited a long, tense moment. "Don't make me beg, Ty."

He shook his head in denial. "I'd never make you beg, Amanda. I was just wondering if I should let you in, considering the gossip. I told you before I don't want to be a party to sullying your name. I meant it."

"I knew all that coming here. I came anyhow. We have to talk, Ty."

Another long, tense moment passed. Then he unlatched the screen door and held it open for her. "Come on in."

"Were you busy?" Now that she was here, in his house, she was losing her nerve. She wanted to turn around and leave, run down the steps and get in her car and go back to the safety of her house and her life.

"I was just getting ready to take a shower."

"It's a good thing I caught you then. I would have gone home in a few minutes."

He smiled. "Relax, Amanda, I'm not going to ravish you."

"No?" She smiled, too. "Too bad."

Ty laughed then, his eyes sparkling with amusement. "I don't really think you mean that."

"No, I don't. I am nervous, awfully nervous," she admitted, shoving her hands in her pockets. She didn't know what to do with them. "And it's not just the gossip. Do you know how hard it is for a Pearson to admit to being wrong?"

"No, but I know how hard it is for a Marshall to admit to being wrong. So I guess I can sympathize, and you might not be wrong, either," he pointed out. "We haven't gotten to the issue yet." He gestured to the sofa. "Make yourself at home. Want something to drink?"

"No, thank you."

"Sure? I've got four gallons of homemade lemonade sitting in the refrigerator."

She smiled. "You must have a mighty thirst. Let me guess, Miss Gertrude, Miss Mabel, Mrs. Crowley, and my Aunt Sophie."

"Almost right. Only the fourth gallon is from the lady whose little girl had the measles. Miss Mabel bakes me cookies. It's my own fault. I should never have mentioned the stuff."

"Not in Rialto, anyhow."

She glanced around the room. The place was lovely, from the rough-hewn grayish paneling interspersed with mirrors on the wall to the oak floors polished to a deep glow to the Early American style furnishings. He'd cleaned and painted and resurfaced. Refurnished. Everything looked comfortable, homey.

"Did you do all this yourself?"

He glanced around proudly. "Every bit."

"It's nice." She gestured to an empty wall. "All you need is a cross-stitched picture for decoration."

"Miss Mabel is working on one for me."

"Oh, I see." Amanda didn't know what else to say.

Ty sat across from her. He had been reading. He tossed a law journal out of the way. "They haven't started the fireworks yet."

"No," Amanda said. "Pretty soon, though. It's almost fully dark."

"Jack Cameron's remarried." The words fell into the room like a gavel hitting a desk. When she glanced at him, her heart thudding with anxiety, he went on talking, his tone soft and gentle, "I thought we'd better jump right in. That's what you want to talk about, isn't it?"

She nodded. "Yes."

"So do I."

"Where do we begin?"

Ty shrugged. "Perhaps with why you think I deceived you. I'd really like to know."

She leaned forward. How could she explain? "I wish I could make you understand, Ty. I don't know if I understand myself. I just feel like—you never told me that you knew about the genetic porphyria."

"I couldn't tell you. I tried to explain that to you the other day. At first I was bound by my commitment to my client, and then, when you read that article and came to me, I knew if I told you that I had known all along that Jack had genetic porphyria, you would think that I was leading you along, feeding you the information."

"Were you?"

"No."

"You didn't help me find that magazine article?"

"It was your journal, Amanda."

"You made me feel like a fool on the witness stand."

"I'm sorry. I was just being dramatic, trying to point out to the jury how the disease worked. I guess I overdid things a bit."

"I felt like a fool for more reasons than drama, Ty. When I got up on the witness stand I realized that we were lovers, and that it would come out. I was angry that you didn't prepare me for that. You could have warned me."

He nodded. "I agree. I was wrong there, Amanda. I should have mentioned it. You were so naive. I know that now. But I thought that if you were appraised of the ramifications, you might back out. As I told you before, winning that case meant a great deal to me."

"You knew you were getting the appointment." It wasn't a question, but a statement of fact.

He nodded again. "Yes, I knew. I never made a secret of that, though. I told you."

"Perhaps in passing."

"Amanda, I had worked toward that end for years. You knew it."

"I didn't think you'd leave."

He kept studying her, his eyes searching her face for the truth. "But my leaving's not the issue, is it?"

"No. It was winning the case."

"Amanda, you have to know that I didn't want to win the case just because of the appointment."

"Why did you want to win, Ty?"

"Because I truly believed in Jack Cameron's innocence. I still believe in his innocence, just like I believe in Tommy Whittiker's innocence. I'm committed to my clients. I always have been, and I always will be."

"All right." That was admirable. She was committed to her patients. "Ty, why did you take Tommy's case?"

"Because I suspected he didn't run his friend down, and because you were here. Now that I've met him, I know he didn't run his friend down, and you're still here."

The fireworks display had started. Amanda could hear the booming in the background. "That night—the first night we met—you wanted me to testify for you. You asked if I would give expert testimony."

"But you refused."

She took a deep breath. She had to face it. "You knew then, didn't you?"

"About Jack's illness? Yes."

"Is that why you pursued me?"

For a moment he didn't answer. Then he said softly, "Yes. At first."

Although the words hurt, she refused to cry. She swallowed the lump in her throat and started to stand up, wanting to run out the door. Ty grasped her hands and pulled her back down.

"Sit down, Amanda. Listen to me." Still holding her hands in his, he knelt in front of her. The look on his face was earnest, pleading. "At first I pursued you because I thought you could help me, or at least give me some information. I believed in Jack's innocence. I owed him the very best defense I could give him. I owe that to all my clients. I came to the hospital that night and I paged you, and then we started seeing each other and I fell in love with you. I still love you."

"Ty, it was wrong."

"No, Amanda, there was nothing wrong about it. Maybe at first it was wrong, I don't know. I shouldn't have tried to use you. But there was nothing wrong with your testimony or with our relationship. The only thing wrong was how I handled things when you came to me and offered to testify, and even then, I didn't do anything ethically or morally wrong. Neither did you. You have to remember, Jack Cameron was innocent. Your testimony set him free."

"Ty, I've felt like—" How could she make him understand? How could she explain? "I've felt so guilty. I don't know if I testified for you because I loved you or because I truly believed Jack had porphyria."

He paused, considering. Then he asked softly, "Amanda, I think we have a problem here. Whose ethics are you questioning, mine or yours?"

Unfortunately he'd asked the key question, the one question she hadn't wanted to face. The question she had avoided these past two years, and would continue to avoid if she could. It was time to admit the truth. "I—mine. I'm questioning my ethics."

He sighed, but it was an expression of sympathy rather than frustration, and he squeezed her hand gently. "I wish I could decide that for you, Amanda, but you have to live with yourself. You have to decide."

"I can't, Ty."

"You have a copy of the chart. Read it."

"What if I'm guilty? What if I'm guilty of violating my professional ethics?" It would destroy her. She got up and walked to the window, watching the fireworks explode in the air. Huge bursts of red, white, and blue. Green. A star. A flag. "I couldn't stand it."

She was already being torn apart by wondering.

Ty had come up behind her. He placed his hands on her shoulders in a gesture of support. As he spoke, his breath whispered along her neck, soft and warm. "The most wonderful thing about you is your sense of right and wrong, your fairness. I'm sorry if I've caused you such torment." Then pausing, he added, "If I had known, I would have turned you down. I would have sacrificed anything to have kept you from being hurt. I thought you knew that, Amanda."

She turned to face him, touched by his admission. "Ty—"

"I love you, Mandy. I'd do anything for you. Anytime, anywhere, anyway."

"Oh, Ty." She was almost in tears.

"Don't cry." He brushed the moisture from her cheeks with his thumb. It was rough against her skin, yet sensuous.

She buried her head in his shoulder. "I've been wrong, haven't I?"

"We've both been wrong."

"Can we make it right?"

"I don't know. I hope so. I've been waiting for you to make that decision."

"I'd like to try." As she drew back to look at him, he cupped her cheeks with his hands, brushing back a wisp of her hair, holding her and studying her face almost reverently. She placed her hands on his, kissing his fingers as they caressed her lips. "Will you kiss me?"

"I'm afraid, Amanda. If I kiss you, I won't stop."

"I don't want to stop."

"What about the gossip? People know you're here." The whole town was at the celebration, but they knew.

"It's time I stood up to them, isn't it?"

"All right." Ty dropped his hands and went to turn off the light. As he flicked the switch she could hear thunder in the distance, the storm moving in. Darkness surrounded them. The phone rang, but he picked it up and recradled it. "You have your beeper, don't you, in case the hospital needs you?"

"Yes. Do you think it might have been an emergency for you?"

"No. It was somebody checking on us. You're sure about this, Amanda?"

She nodded. "Yes."

He held out his hand. "Then let's go. I'll show you what I've done with the bedroom."

They walked arm in arm up the steps. Since he didn't turn on the lights, Amanda didn't see much of the bedroom at all. The storm was moving in, though, and lightning illuminated the room in fiery streaks. When he closed the door she turned toward him. "We're going to get some rain."

"Maybe it will cool the temperature down. It's been hot."

"Maybe." She stood still as he closed the window shades and walked toward her.

"Doubts?"

"Only about myself. It's been a long time."

"Yes," he agreed, "a very long time. Over two years."

"Have you made love to anyone else?"

"No."

She was surprised at his answer. Pleased. "Neither have I."

"Remember the first time?"

"Oh, yes." They'd made love in front of his fireplace, the pretend one. Yet she would swear that she had seen the flames flicker. "In a way I feel like this is the first time."

Certainly her heart was pounding like the first time. Her stomach quivered in anticipation, fear that she might be inadequate and her breathing was shaky.

"So do I," he murmured.

She wasn't certain which one of them was delaying the moment, her or Ty. He kept moving toward her, slowly, deliberately. Just watching him her skin felt hot and flushed, as though a fiery blaze was smoldering inside her.

"Can you feel it?" he asked huskily. "I can still feel the fire."

"Oh, yes, I feel it."

Now he was directly in front of her, standing there but still not touching her. "I want you, Amanda, with every fiber of my being. I love you."

"I love you, Ty."

Then he touched her cheek, lightly, moving his hand down along her throat, and stepped closer. The storm outside moved in quickly. She could hear the thunder and lightning crash around her as he murmured, "Let's light the fire again."

He lowered his lips to hers. For all their hesitation, all it took was one touch, one brush of his mouth against hers, and she was in his arms and he was kissing her with all the pent-up emotion of a man who had waited two years to touch the woman he loved. Drawing a ragged breath, Ty crushed her against his hard length. Amanda slumped against him, reveling in the feel of him next to her, the lash-hard muscles holding her, the need that surged against her thighs.

She wasn't certain when they took their clothes off, or even how. Before she knew it her things were lying in a heap on the floor and she was naked, pressed against him. Because they knew what was coming they could hardly wait. There was no gentleness between them. Each kiss, each caress became a harsh, savage embrace. Ty's hands tormented her, his lips traumatized her, his voice mesmerized her.

"Mandy," he murmured, "sweet, sweet Mandy."

A sharp, delicious ache throbbed inside her as his lips sought and tortured the tender flesh of her breasts, his teeth grazing her erect nipples. She thrust toward him, no longer cognizant of the world, only of the two of them, together. She felt as though the storm had intensified into a raging, swirling force, buffeting and whirling her into another universe—another time, only the storm was inside her, and it was Ty.

They could wait no longer. Lying her on the bed he possessed her. Amanda climaxed immediately, gasping with wild, sweet agony. But Ty started to slowly stroke her again, the powerful aphrodisiac of his touch making her moan with renewed desire, returning her to the raging fervor of unrestrained need.

His hands were everywhere on her body, kneading, brushing, trailing a searing brand across her naked flesh. His lips followed, hot and soft and moist all at the same time. He explored the dips and hollows of her body with an expert touch, a remembered touch, bringing her to the brink of surrender and back, forward and back, until she wanted to cry out with frustration. She thrashed beneath him, tossing her head from side to side. Her body was damp from perspiration, from the smoldering need that coursed through her veins with his every caress.

"Ty! Oh, Tyler!" she cried as his tongue discovered the secret place inside her. Her body throbbed. "Please . . ."

"What, Mandy? What do you want?" Torturing her more, he flicked his tongue over and over the quivering peak. "Say it, Mandy." It was a husky command. "Tell me what you want."

The depth of her emotions didn't allow Amanda to speak. She arched her hips toward him, begging him with her body, but he would have no part of it.

"Say it, Mandy. Tell me you want me."

"Oh, God, love me. Love me now," she cried.

"You're beautiful, Mandy," he murmured huskily, his voice shivering through her, "so very beautiful."

"Ty!" she gasped when he at last claimed her. She wrapped her arms around him, joyously matching his rhythmic movements with a wanton abandon that shocked even her. Never, never had she felt this way with a man, except for him. *Ty,* her mind cried. *Ty, I love you.*

Soon, coherent thoughts fled her mind as need overwhelmed her. All she could think of was the feel of him inside her. As the storm outside raged, thrashing rain against the windows, the one in her body heightened, then peaked. Wave after wave of pleasure ripped through her in undulating ripples, surging, welling, soaring, until she collapsed in exhausted ecstasy.

* * *

Afterward he gathered her to him, kissing her lightly on her lips, the tip of her nose, her forehead, her hairline. They didn't speak. Words weren't necessary. He held her for the longest time. Her limbs felt languid and lifeless and she rested her head on his shoulder. Outside the storm had abated, too. Rain fell lightly against the window pane.

When at last she could move, she explored his body freely, trailing her hands along his powerful shoulders, down the hard flesh of his back and arms, delighting in the feel of him, in the form and texture of him. Once she had memorized every pore of his flesh, now she re-explored it, learning it all over again, gaining intimate knowledge of every cell of his body. There were callouses on his hands that hadn't been there before, a scar on his back from minor surgery, a tiny mole on the inside of his thigh.

"You're playing with fire, Amanda," he said when she brushed her hand over him lightly.

"Me? Whatever do you mean?"

"This." In one quick, lithe movement, he reversed their positions and kissed her. They made love again, this time slowly and leisurely, learning and marveling at each other's bodies, and saddened by all the time they had missed. Then they showered and ate and talked some more.

Later that night, Ty handed her his copy of the chart she had tucked in her file cabinet two years ago, and as she read, she knew without a doubt that she had done the right thing. While it was true that the only evidence of a genetic illness was still flimsy—a simple urine test, porphyria was the only thing that made sense. Nine out of ten doctors would agree with her. It was time to stop worrying about that tenth opinion, and concentrate on the future instead of the past.

The future was now, here, and it was Ty.

Chapter Eight

ALTHOUGH THE ENTIRE TOWN knew that Amanda had spent the night with Ty, no one mentioned it directly. However, the next morning she was swamped with a lot of indirect inquiries. Mrs. Crowley was out pulling weeds when Amanda came home.

"Well, hello, Mandy," the woman called the moment she pulled into the driveway, "quite a storm we had last night."

"Yes," Amanda agreed, getting out of her car. "It doesn't seem to have done much for the heat, though."

"Nearly ruined the fireworks. An hour earlier and we wouldn't have had such a fitting end to our celebration. Did you happen to catch the display?"

No sense in denying it. The woman knew she hadn't. "No, I left early."

"Someone sick?"

Amanda couldn't help flushing. "No. Mr. Marshall and I had some things to discuss."

"And how did that go?"

Amanda flushed deeper. "Fine."

"How did he like your lunch?" she kept probing. "Did he ever find some lemonade?"

"Yes, plenty. Yours was especially good."

"Why, thank you, Mandy." Mrs. Crowley smiled, obviously pleased by the compliment. "Zeke likes my lemonade, too. But don't worry, I don't let him have any sugar with it. I know he has to watch his diet."

"Good." Amanda started for her house. "Well, I have to go inside now. I'll see you later."

"Oh, Mandy." Apparently Mrs. Crowley wasn't going to give up. "Did you say you and Mr. Marshall have worked out your differences?"

Amanda paused. She hadn't said. "Yes, we did."

"Well, then, what are his intentions?"

"I don't know," Amanda said. "Do you?"

"Why, no." For the first time since Amanda had known Mrs. Crowley, the woman flushed. "I hope you don't think I was being nosy, dear."

Amanda smiled. "Not at all. I do have to go."

She got inside and the phone was ringing. Three calls later Sheriff Toombs came by to collect on his bet. Or at least Amanda assumed that's what he was trying to do. She was surprised to see him at the door. He'd almost blurted out that she needed to pay off when he must have realized what he'd be implying, for he turned red and shifted from one foot to the other. "Well, how you doing these days, Mandy Lou?" he asked instead, folding the brim of his hat in his hands.

"Great. How are you?"

"Fine. Feelin' fine."

Amanda waited. "Is there something you wanted, Sheriff Toombs?"

"No, just came by to say hello. How's Tyler?"

"Good."

"He still seein' Tommy?"

"I suppose."

"Don't you talk about it?"

"No," Amanda admitted honestly. They'd had an awful lot of other stuff to discuss.

"Trial's comin' up soon."

She nodded. "Yes, I know."

"You gonna testify?"

The question of the decade. Funny, all this time she'd thought Ty had been trying to convince her to testify for him. "Do you still need me?"

"Prosecutor does. He figures you can give the results of the blood-alcohol level."

"Fine, I'll be there. Was that all?"

"Yes, ma'am." He kept shifting uncomfortably. "Say hello to Tyler for me. You seein' him tonight?"

"I hope so. By the way," she said, figuring she may as well get it over with, "don't I owe you some money? We had a bet, didn't we?"

He actually turned red again. "Don't worry about it, Mandy. That was just in fun." He lowered his voice. "An' really, he ain't won the Whittiker case yet, you know."

She smiled. "No, he hasn't. Not yet." But she had every confidence that he would win, and soon.

After Sheriff Toombs left Amanda had several more phone calls, including one from Jean Renee, who was as happy as Amanda about the evening's events. Amanda didn't tell her friend that she and Ty had made love; she didn't have to. Jean knew it. "Did you work out your differences?"

Another universal question. Everyone seemed to want to know the answer. "I think so. We talked a lot."

"I'll bet."

"We did," Amanda objected.

"Good, I'm glad you've finally cleared the air. I like Ty."

"So do I."

"Actually, so does the whole town. But there goes the topic of speculation. Now what are we going to talk about?"

"Birth control?" Amanda suggested. "Your using it."

"I'll be good, Mandy. I promise. No more babies after this one."

Amanda was surprised. "What convinced you?"

"The wedding dresses. No, seriously, Dan and I discussed it and he's getting worried about me. You know what a rough time I had with the last one."

"I know." Amanda had delivered the child, and it had been a touch and go situation.

"Dan didn't realize I wasn't using anything. He says we can take in foster children if I'd like. Or we could adopt. I just have this thing about babies."

"That's because you haven't had a bad one yet. I don't know why they all sleep for you. Other mothers tell me their children are up day and night."

"I guess I've been lucky. But so have you," Jean switched the subject. "So tell me all about it. What's going on? Are you and Tyler an item?"

Amanda laughed, unable to keep the excitement from her voice. "I certainly hope so."

The town gossip grapevine didn't fail this time around either. Amanda juggled similar questions throughout the day—when she went on rounds, when she had office hours, even at the hospital. The nurses all thought she'd made a fine choice. Inez still didn't have an opinion.

Amanda felt like the lone fish in a fish bowl. In a way, it was kind of fun to be the center of attention. She was supposed to see Ty that night, only she didn't know if she was ever going to get through the day. Around four she was called to the baseball field to treat an injured player. She was supposed to meet Ty for dinner at five, but that would have to wait.

The Little League baseball team played at the same park where they'd held the Fourth of July festival the day before. Amazingly the grounds were cleaned up; there wasn't a scrap of garbage to be found. The ground was slightly damp from last night's rain. Amanda got out of her car and hurried across the park. She hated injuries, treating them with just simple first aid. One of these days she was going to talk the town fathers into getting an ambulance and paramedics. But for now she was all they had. Several players had gathered around the injured player, who happened to be Ty.

He sat on the ground in the middle of a group of laughing teens, waiting for her. Amanda rushed to his side. "Ty, what happened? Are you all right?"

"I'm fine," he said, grinning at her, "I just have a little scrape."

She frowned. "A little scrape? Then why did you call me?"

"I couldn't wait to see you."

"Ty."

He grinned again, and she felt herself softening. "Don't worry," he said, "I knew you didn't have any other patients. I told the kids to ask Inez if you were doing anything before they called you out."

Talk about standing up to someone. She pursed her lips and put on her most professional demeanor, trying to steel herself to his charm. "But are you hurt or not?"

"I told you, I have a little scrape."

She glanced at his arm. If the scrape was any smaller it would be minuscule. "What happened?"

"I slid into the base."

All the kids were standing around in a circle, watching and smiling. This whole thing had been a setup. But why? "Ty, what are you doing here?"

"Here?" He gestured around at the ball field.

"Yes."

"I thought I'd see where my money was going to. You know I donated a thousand dollars to this team."

She nodded. "Yes, I know."

"I decided to play a few innings."

"And you got hurt."

"Yes."

"But not bad."

"I wanted to see you," he said. "I couldn't wait." He swept out his arm to include the ball team. "Meet the Mandylou's."

Amanda stared at the teenaged boys all standing around in T-shirts and jeans. When they turned around she saw her name emblazoned on their backs. "They're naming a baseball team after me?"

Ty nodded. "Isn't it neat?"

"I think it's silly." She laughed. "The Mandylou's? It sounds like a rock group."

"Thanks. It was my idea, Amanda."

"I'm sorry."

"Aren't you touched?"

"Yes, I am," she said sincerely. "Thank you," she said to the boys. "I hope you have a good season."

They inundated her with numbers and averages and promises of play-offs. When they were finished, she started to pick up her medical bag and leave.

"Wait a minute," Ty said. "Where are you going?"

"Did you want something?"

"You."

She gave a sidelong glance at the boys. "I have some things to do."

"What about my scrape?"

She stared at his arm a moment. Then she handed him a Band-Aid. "Here. Put this on. I'll see you for dinner. By the way, what are you cooking?"

"Me?" he queried. "I can't cook."

"Neither can I. Surely you didn't forget?"

Ty was stunned. He sat on the ground with his mouth agape. "You've been back here for two years and you haven't learned how to cook? Mandy, all small-town women know how to cook. It's inherent in their genes."

"Then I have a genetic defect." She waved and started for her car. "Thanks again."

That night when Ty picked her up he didn't mention the Mandylou's, but he had the Band-Aid she'd given him on a string, tied around his rearview mirror. She got in the car and frowned at it. "What is that?"

"A Band-Aid."

"I realize that," Amanda said. "What's the meaning of it?"

"Don't you know? All the teenaged boys have a memento of their love hanging from their mirror. Dice or a garter." He pretended to adjust the Band-Aid. "This is mine. It's the only thing you've ever given me."

She shook her head in disbelief. "You're crazy, Ty."

"True." He leaned over to kiss her. "Crazy in love."

They went to dinner at the café on Main Street that night and the night after that and the night after that. Amanda was in love, too. She saw Ty at every available moment. They went to baseball games, rooting her team on, and out for drives. She had to show him every inch of the countryside. The man had a fetish not only for lemonade, but for making love in little out-of-the-way spots. Amanda was always afraid they would get caught, but Ty seemed to delight in tempting fate, and in tempting her. Or rather, in teasing her. They were out driving one night when he pulled in at the bluff.

"What are you doing?" Amanda asked.

"Going to Lover's Lane."

She glanced at him. "Ty! We're adults."

"So?"

"Adults don't go to Lover's Lane."

"Really?" He parked the car and got out. Since it was early they were the only ones there. "Come on," he said, taking her hand, "let's go down by the river. I've finally figured out what those settlers must have thought when they got here."

To say Amanda was puzzled would be an understatement. She frowned. "What are you talking about, Ty?"

"I figure they got here in the summer, too, when it

was hot," he went on, helping her down the embankment, "and I'd be willing to bet they abandoned their wagons and went skinny-dipping in the river."

Skinny-dipping? She stared at him. "Ty, you're not going to do this."

He stood on the riverbank nodding. "Absolutely. Doesn't it look inviting?"

"Everyone will know."

He glanced around. "No one's here."

"They'll still know," Amanda said. "Ty, this is a small town. The night of the Fourth of July festival every single person who lives in Rialto was at the celebration. Yet the next day Inez asked me why I was playing Morse code with the lights. Someone saw us flicking the lights on and off."

"Do you mind?"

"That's not the point."

"Sure it is."

"All right," she conceded. "I don't mind, but I'm not going to take my clothes off and jump naked in a river just to prove it."

"So leave some clothes on," he suggested, a devilish grin lighting his face. "I hear that's sexier. Don't you think it's hot out?"

It was sweltering. The heat wave hadn't broken at all. "There are other ways to get cool, Ty."

"Name them."

"Ice water."

"Right here. A whole river full." Still grinning, he gestured to the water. "Amanda, the kids come down here during the day and swim all the time," he went on, trying to convince her. "I see them constantly. And what do you think happens here when the cars start pulling in? I'll bet it's not just hugs and kisses and hands in the backseat. Two to one this river gets a lot of use."

Amanda had already made one bad bet. She wasn't going to make another. Not that she doubted his claim. She just wasn't certain she was ready to have the rumors spread all over town that she had used said river—with Ty. Of course, she wasn't certain what the difference was, the rumors about them were already hot and heavy.

Yet the townsfolk still adored him. Every single person seemed pleased at the new turn of events. Ty and Amanda were spoken of in the same breath. Frank was the only dark spot in their happiness, but even he was dating someone new, and there was already talk of plans for the future—something that hadn't been mentioned when they were dating.

"You're sure you want to do this?" Amanda asked, watching as Ty started to strip off his shirt and pants.

"I'm sure."

She glanced around at the dark night, the trees that shaded the area. The bluff seemed so secluded. The moon was a silvery sliver in the sky, hardly illuminating the area at all, just reflecting a thin strip on the river. Yet she knew someone would see her. "Are you going to take everything off?"

"Why not?"

She turned away, embarrassed. "Because I'll see you."

He laughed. "Then I'll leave my pants on. Come on."

"Wait a minute."

Amanda pulled back as Ty dove in the water. He surfaced, sputtering, and shook the moisture from his hair. "Oh, it's cold! Come on in, Mandy," he shouted. "It's great."

"Shhh," she said, looking around, still not sure that they were alone. In Rialto no one was ever alone. She took her sandal off and dipped her toe in the water. "It's cold, Ty."

"Yes, but it's great. Just jump in all at once."

She was wearing a sundress and she kept glancing around as she pulled it off, knowing someone would see her. "I don't know. I think this is a mistake, Ty."

"I'll hold you and keep you warm."

"I thought the purpose was to get cool."

He laughed again. "The purpose is to kiss you, Miss Amanda Louise Pearson."

She stuck her tongue out at him. "You can do that without tempting me into the water, Mr. Gordon Tyler Marshall."

"But I'm in the water."

Even though she had left her brassiere and panties on, Amanda gave one final glance around the area before she dropped her dress and dove into the river. The cold was brief, but shocking. She hissed her breath inward and shivered as Ty swam toward her.

"See," he said, grabbing her around the waist and swinging her toward him, "isn't it great?"

"Super." Even her teeth chattered.

He kissed her on the nose, teasing her. "Warmer?"

"Hardly."

Now that she had adjusted to the water temperature, she did think it was nice, and she started to tread water beside him. "Ty, did you ever go skinny-dipping for real?"

"Do you want me to take off my shorts?"

"No!" she said, horrified.

"Why not?"

"Because we're out in public." While they were in a river in private, to Amanda they were really out in public.

"Didn't you do this as a kid?"

"No. I was a good little girl. I only told lies."

"You know, Mandy, you're really prudish. It must be your upbringing."

"Must be."

"Let's give it a test." Ty took her in his arms, planting tiny kisses along her mouth and down her throat, each brush of his lips longer and more lingering than the last. When she giggled he kissed her some more, moving down to her breasts.

Amanda gasped. Desire surged through her veins, hot and hard, and she felt suddenly weak. She could feel her nipples peak. "Ty," she murmured.

"Very prudish." Still kissing her, he drew one hand up her thigh in a caress. The water made everything more sensual, seductive.

She moaned, thrusting closer to him.

Taking a ragged breath he said, "Come on, let's go home."

But Amanda was in a silly mood. She pulled back. "I thought you were hot, Ty."

"I am," he murmured, "that's the problem."

She laughed and swam away. "Come on, it's cooler over here."

"You're teasing me, aren't you?"

"Mmm-hmm."

"Wait until I get my hands on you."

"Promises, promises."

"Darn you, woman." Ty started chasing Amanda through the water. She giggled and swam away. They were dodging and laughing and having a great time when a car pulled in and lights flashed on them.

Amanda felt as if she'd been caught with her hand in the cookie jar. She stopped swimming and glanced at the hillside. "Damn," she muttered.

"Don't worry," Ty said, "it's probably just some kids here to make out."

A car door opened and closed. "Hey; Doc!" somebody called. "Mandy Lou?"

She sighed when she recognized Jimmy John's voice. "A kid?"

Ty shrugged. "What do you think he wants?"

"I don't know."

"Mandy Lou?" Jimmy John called again. "Mandy Lou, is that you out there?"

"Yes," she called back, swimming toward the shore. "It's me. What's the matter?"

"You don't have to hurry. Take your time."

She didn't bother to ask how he'd known where to find her. She was just worried that her beeper didn't work. She should have heard the page from the water. Hurriedly she pulled her sundress on over her wet, dripping body and climbed up the bank. "What's wrong? Is someone sick?"

"What are you doing in the water?"

"Swimming."

"Oh." Jimmy John itched his arm. "Sorry to bother you, Doc, but I think I got the measles."

For a moment Amanda wasn't certain she heard him right. She stared at him. "The measles?"

"Yes, ma'am."

Somehow it seemed fitting.

Ty had climbed out of the water behind Amanda, pulling on his pants. When he heard what the old man said he turned away. Amanda could tell he was trying not to laugh. "What is it that you want me to do about it, Jimmy John?" she asked.

He stared at her as though he didn't understand. "What else? I want you to fix me. You're the doc."

Amanda prescribed some medication for his itching and left strict instructions for him to go to bed and stay there for at least a week. Several other people thought they might catch the measles, too, but she assured them it wasn't an epidemic, Jimmy John had never had the measles before. Most of the children over the age of a year had been immunized. Even the little girl who had caught them to begin with had had the shot. Occasionally it failed, but that didn't mean everyone else was going to get sick. Everything was going to be fine.

Ty seemed to take it all in stride. He didn't even mind that they had been caught swimming nude—or nearly nude. Whenever he could, he embellished the story with a wild tale of his own, a tale of witches and goblins and demons from outer space. Listening to him Amanda was struck with the sudden realization that if he asked her to go to Mars she'd ask where she could catch the nearest space shuttle. She did feel sorry for the town, though. One night, after he'd teased the waitress at the café mercilessly, she tried to reason with him.

They walked down the block hand in hand, headed for his car. "You shouldn't lead them on this way, Ty."

"Why not? They know it's a game."

Was it a game with her? She shouldn't have doubts,

but she did. "Ty," she asked thoughtfully, "are you happy here?"

He glanced at her with a frown. "Why wouldn't I be happy? I'm with you."

"But there's nothing to challenge you. You play handyman and you look at an occasional tractor warranty."

"I do more than that, Amanda."

"What?"

"I have Tommy's case and just the other day Miss Mabel had me draw up her will."

"Big deal. How long did it take, ten minutes?"

"That wasn't nice."

"Look, I didn't mean to be nasty," she went on, "I just meant that the kinds of cases you get here in Rialto can't possibly compare with the things you would do in Chicago or New York."

"I told you when I came here that I was tired of the big city. Didn't you believe me?"

It wasn't that she didn't believe him, exactly, it was just that it seemed too good to be true. Why would a dynamic lawyer like Ty be content in a small town like Rialto, Illinois? "I guess I'm just being overly anxious."

"Don't borrow trouble, Mandy." He kissed her lightly on the forehead. "I like Rialto, and I love you."

She smiled at him. "I love you, too."

The problem, she had finally realized, was that she loved him too much.

Chapter Nine

FOR THE NEXT TWO weeks they settled into a routine of sorts. During the day, while Ty worked on Tommy Whittiker's case, Amanda saw her patients. At night they would eat dinner together and then relax at either her house or his. Although they still laughed and fooled around, skinny-dipping in the river or driving to secluded out-of-the-way spots to make love, the closer it came to the trial date, the more preoccupied Ty became. Amanda remembered he'd been that way with the Jack Cameron case, too. It was as though his energies were devoted to one thing, and one thing only. That was probably what made him such a terrific defense attorney.

But he'd been working for several hours now, since early afternoon. They'd skipped dinner. Amanda had cut up some fruit and cheese, and they'd just snacked. Still Ty had sat at his desk, concentrating. He looked so tired. She went to where he sat, writing on a yellow legal pad, and started to massage his shoulders. "Almost done?"

He glanced up at her and smiled. "Almost. Want to go for a ride?"

"No," she said. "I was just beginning to worry about you. I'm a doctor, you know, and you don't look very good."

He smiled again, and placed down his pen. "I'm fine. Just trying to get my thoughts straight for my opening statement. It's only a couple of days away, you know."

The impending trial was the topic of conversation these days. Amanda had discharged both boys from the hospital last week. Tommy was staying with his grandparents in Rialto. Bobby Martin had gone home to his folks in Senton.

"Yes, I know. Have you figured out a defense yet?" she asked. He'd been working toward that end for several days now.

Ty sighed and got up from the desk. "No. Or at least I haven't come up with anything yet that's going to clear Tommy of the charges. In fact, I should talk to him again, see if I can get any more information from him. Do you mind?"

"Now?" Amanda shrugged. "No, I don't mind."

"Want to come along for the ride?"

"Is that ethical?"

He grinned at her. "Still worried about ethics?"

"Not really. I just wondered."

"You're his doctor, aren't you?"

Ty had a good point. "I'll get a sweater. Is Tommy still refusing to talk?"

"Not so much refusing," Ty explained, "as just not having anything to say. You know, most of my clients have too much to say on the subject of their guilt or innocence. Tommy is a real challenge." She got her sweater and Ty helped her on with it. "It's hot out, Amanda. Are you sure you want to wear this?"

"I hear it's going to rain again."

"Don't count on it. They've forecast the heat wave continuing for well into next week. You're getting as bad as Miss Mabel, carrying around a coat all the time."

"Thanks." But Amanda laughed. In a way she *was* becoming entrenched in the ways of the small town. And so was Ty. Just yesterday he'd bought a rocking chair for his front porch.

Since Amanda liked to ride in the Mercedes with the windows down, they didn't turn on the air-conditioning. She leaned her head back against the seat as they drove out of town toward the Whittiker farm. Glenn and Eunice had come for the trial, but they were staying at a hotel in Effingham. Tommy was still with his grandparents. Although it was dark out, the ride was pleasant. The buds on the trees had closed for the night and most of the livestock had wandered to barns or sheds to be bedded down. Except for the normal nighttime sounds, everything was quiet.

"How are the winters here?" Ty asked suddenly.

Amanda turned toward him. Sometimes he asked the oddest questions at the oddest times. "Cold. Snowy."

"Do you like snow?"

"When I don't have to drive in it."

"That's pretty much a universal attitude. I like snow. It's a puzzle to me."

"A puzzle you can't defend." She smiled at him.

Ty smiled back. "Sure I can. Are you making fun of me, Amanda?"

"No."

"Tommy says he didn't like to take his motorcycle through the snow."

Amanda frowned. "So?"

"It was raining when he ran into Mary Cahill's pigpen. Jimmy John said the place was a sea of mud. That's kind of like snow, isn't it?"

Amanda shrugged. "I don't know. What are you getting at, Ty?"

He sighed. "I wish I knew myself. For some reason it just doesn't make sense to me that someone would run into a pigpen on purpose. Even a teenager."

"He was showing off."

"Maybe. Maybe not."

"He was going home. He didn't have any choice except to ride in the mud."

"But the roads weren't muddy. Just the pigpen."

Amanda frowned in confusion. "Maybe he saw the mud and couldn't resist."

When Ty gave her a skeptical glance, she laughed.

"All right," she admitted. "That was a little dumb. I don't have any other theories. You certainly have put in a lot of work on this case, Ty. Do you always research so carefully?"

He nodded. "That's how I win."

But Tommy didn't offer any more light on that subject or on any other subject. He kept saying he couldn't remember or he didn't know. Even Amanda could tell there were things he didn't want to discuss. The teenaged boy sat at his grandparents' kitchen table and shook his head, as though confused, indecisive. "I simply don't remember," he said when Ty asked him again about the evening's events. "I wish I could."

Amanda had always like Tommy. He'd been a spoiled little rich kid when he'd come here to live, but he'd soon changed. He was an attractive boy, tall and lean with dark hair and dark, flashing eyes. Though Tommy had a brooding sensitivity that she felt certain was sincere, he needed a few more years to grow up.

"What are you going to do now?" Amanda asked Ty when they left.

He shrugged. "The best I can, I guess."

"Why are you so sure he's innocent?"

Ty glanced at her. "Do you think he's guilty?"

Amanda wasn't certain. Everything was so muddled. "I'm not sure."

"Neither am I anymore," Ty admitted. "For some reason—and for the life of me I can't say why—I believe the boy."

"Blind faith?"

"Maybe. I don't know. Don't get me wrong, I don't have to believe in him to defend him. Everybody, no matter how low, deserves some kind of defense. That's how our legal system is based. But I keep thinking that there's something about Tommy that makes me want to trust my instincts."

"Have you ever done that before?"

"Plenty of times."

"Have you ever been wrong?"

He laughed. "More times than I've been right. But regardless, I still trust my instincts. Most lawyers do."

"Is that smart?"

"Believe me, Amanda, sometimes it's all you have."

* * *

For the next few days Ty operated on instinct exclusively. When the trial started, he became busier and busier. She saw very little of him. What time she did spend with him, he was wrapped up in the case. She had been called in by the prosecution and she had given her testimony, though it was short and needless. She had expected Ty to be brutal with his cross-examination, but he had had hardly anything to say to her, except for something minor that ended up being ruled as speculation.

The evening of the fourth day, Ty was exhausted. The heat wave had continued and the courthouse air-conditioning broke down. To top it off, true to Amanda's prediction, the press and wire services had picked up on the case and headlines were being splashed nationwide. For the first time Ty wasn't able to do much for his client. She hated seeing him so despondent.

"The trial's almost over, isn't it?" she guessed that evening as they were watching television.

Ty nodded. "I'll be presenting my closing argument tomorrow afternoon."

"Why aren't you working on it?" She was puzzled. Normally he didn't move from the desk all evening.

"I've already written it. There's not much to say." Although he stared at the television she could tell he wasn't really seeing the screen. That was just as well. Some of the things the news media were saying were downright cruel. There had even been a few articles about Ty and Amanda, but she had ignored them. This time she had testified for the prosecution. "I've finally figured out the problem," Ty went on. "Tommy feels guilty. For some reason he wants to be punished."

"That's silly."

Ty agreed. "You tell him that. I'm tired of trying."

"Did you cross-examine Bobby Martin yet?"

"No. The prosecution didn't put him on the stand. They didn't have to. They had Sandy and all of the kids' arguments."

"Who did you use?"

He glanced at her. "Character witnesses."

"There's nothing you can do, Ty. You tried your best."

"I don't know," he said, getting up to pace the floor. "It seems like I should be able to do something. In normal circumstances this kind of case would get thrown out of court for lack of evidence. Hell, in normal circumstances it wouldn't get to court. I should be winning hands down, and I can't even gather a defense."

The look in his eyes—so sincere, so sad—made Amanda hurt inside. She wanted to comfort him. She stood in front of him and took his hands in hers. "Ty, it's not your fault."

"I know. But I care, Mandy. I care so damned much."

She knew how that felt. She cared about her patients. She cared about him. "I love you, Ty."

He turned her palm over and brought it to his lips with a sad smile. "Thanks, I love you, too." Then he reached to flip off the television and took her hand again. "Come on, let's go to bed."

Throughout the past few weeks, since they'd been back together, Amanda had experienced many facets of lovemaking. It seemed that every time they made love it was with a new emotion. This time it was for support. He needed her. It was that simple. She gave her body freely and wanted nothing more than to help him through the moment. That was the way love should be.

Afterward they fell asleep holding each other. Sometime during the night her beeper went off. Ty wanted to drive her to Parkersville, but she refused.

"It's just someone with a headache," she told him, dressing hurriedly and turning the light back off. "I'll be fine. I'm on call tonight." Because she was on staff at the hospital, every so often she had to be on emergency call. Sometimes she actually enjoyed the change in routine. "You get some sleep. You have to give your closing argument tomorrow."

He didn't seem happy about her choice. "Be careful. Wake me when you get in."

"Will do."

The hospital was typically quiet for a weeknight. A few patients were in the emergency room. The staff apologized for calling her out, but the patient had insisted on seeing an attending physician. Amanda examined the man and administered medication. Two hours later he was fine. She was on her way home when she ran into one of the Intensive Care nurses taking a break.

"How've you been, Dr. Pearson?" the young woman asked.

"Busy."

"I see in the papers that the Martin-Whittiker trial is in full swing."

Amanda nodded. "It's actually almost over."

"It's a shame. They were all nice kids."

"Yes," Amanda agreed.

"Say, did you ever follow up on that incident with Tommy?"

Amanda paused. "What incident?"

"Didn't you see it on the chart? I thought for sure I wrote it in the nurses notes. One night Tommy acted really weird. I came into the room and he was just sitting there, staring. Only it was different. He looked like patients do when they've just had a seizure."

"Did he have a seizure?" Amanda asked, frowning. He hadn't complained of a head injury.

"No," the nurse answered, "not that I ever saw, but that one time he was like a patient who had had one. It's hard to describe. He denied it, of course, said he'd just been sleeping hard. I was just wondering if he happened to have a family history of epilepsy."

"That's a good question."

"Well, I hope they aren't too hard on him. I know he's on trial for attempted murder, but I'd hate to see him in jail. I don't think he meant to hurt that other kid."

It was odd how everyone formed opinions so easily. Amanda wished it were so easy for her. While driving home, Amanda thought of something she couldn't believe she or Ty hadn't thought of before. She could call the local hospital in the town where Eunice and Glenn had moved and request Eunice's medical history. Perhaps it would reveal something that would help Tommy.

When Amanda received the call back from Eunice Whittiker's physician, she couldn't believe what she had heard—Eunice Whittiker had epilepsy. For sure. No doubt. Diagnosed epileptic. That meant Tommy could have the disease, too. Did he even know he might be epileptic? Perhaps he had never had a seizure before.

But sometimes it wasn't the disease that caused the problem, she thought. In this case, the drug that controlled the disease could be the culprit. Quite often alcohol enhanced the effects of drugs. And Tommy liked beer. How ironic. There was every possibility that Tommy Whittiker might have a genetic disease that was causing black-out spells, which in turn, might have caused the accident. It was exactly like the case in Chicago!

Amanda tried to think. The night Tommy had run into Mary Cahill's pigpen he'd been drinking. As Ty had pointed out, no one in his right mind would run into a pigpen on purpose, not even a teenager. What if Tommy had drunk a beer during the night of the accident? One beer was hardly enough to make a difference in his blood-alcohol level, which would explain the low number. Yet it could mess up a drug level, particularly if that drug was used to control seizures.

But why wouldn't Tommy have told her he had epilepsy? Amanda was his doctor. Why hadn't his parents come forward? There was no reason for Amanda to test for the disease. Tommy had to know that. She hadn't taken a drug screen, and epilepsy wouldn't show up in routine blood tests, like the ones he'd had. If only she'd tested for the disease—but there had been no indication.

More to the point, she wondered why Tommy wouldn't tell Ty. The boy was on trial for attempted murder. Surely he wasn't concerned with the stigma still associated with epilepsy? Yet that wasn't a new attitude. It had been Amanda's experience that people would withhold information, vital information, even when it was a life and death situation. Rialto was a small town. That was why Amanda couldn't find Eunice's medical history in her father's files. Eunice had been too embarrassed to go to the town doctor.

All of a sudden, Amanda realized that Eunice was the reason. Tommy was protecting his mother, who wouldn't want anyone to know she had epilepsy. Eunice was from Rialto, but she was from one of the "good families," and it would destroy her to be the topic of gossip. How could she have let her son go to jail? The Whittikers had hired Ty, which was probably how they were figuring to win the case. Amanda had always teased Ty that he could win cases with just his personality. Glenn Whittiker probably didn't even know about his wife's illness.

Amanda sat at her desk wondering what to do. The newspapers had already had a field day with her and Ty. If she was wrong, she would look silly. If she was right . . . Either way, she would have to testify. It was the only chance Tommy had.

Ty was thrilled with her information—thrilled and yet a bit surprised. "Although I don't know why I should be surprised," he said. "I've seen worse."

"Do you think I'm right?"

"About Tommy protecting his mother?" He frowned. "Yes, it does seem logical. We'll know in about an hour. Are you sure you want to do this, Amanda?" he went on. "You realize the press is there."

She nodded. "Yes, I know."

"They know about us."

"Will that hurt your case?"

"It won't help it, but I'm all Tommy has. It would be silly for me to drop out as his defense attorney simply because you have evidence and we have a relationship. I'll tell him, though, and see what he says."

"That is, if you can convince him to let me testify in the first place."

"I'll convince him, Amanda. That's the least of my worries. Now that we have something to work with we can't let him go to jail."

Amanda was curious. "Ty? Did you tell Jack Cameron about us? Did he know there could be publicity?"

He nodded. "Yes. Jack knew. He was willing to risk the innuendoes."

Now she was willing to risk them. At last.

Amanda was right about Tommy protecting his mother. Later that morning both the boy and Eunice broke down when confronted with the truth. And that afternoon, when Amanda took the witness stand, the reporters went wild. The courtroom became such bedlam that the judge had to call for a recess until the morning.

Even though the trial wasn't over, Ty was ecstatic. He knew they'd scored a victory. That night, as they sat in the café on Main Street, it seemed as though every person in town stopped by to congratulate him.

"You know the headlines are going to be brutal," he said to Amanda.

She nodded, amazed they finally had a moment to talk. "Yes, I know."

"You're ready for the gossip?"

Was anyone ever ready for gossip? Particularly the malicious kind that always cropped up in situations like this one. But she knew words couldn't hurt her. Besides, she'd done the right thing.

When they arrived at Ty's house, they heard his phone ring non-stop before he was even able to unlock the front door. Everyone called with congratulations for him, and for Tommy. The only way they got away from the publicity was to go to Amanda's house. But then Mrs. Crowley came over. And Aunt Sophie. And Jimmy John.

They finally turned out the lights and went to bed.

Amanda wasn't needed in court the next morning. She made her rounds as usual, starting with the hospital in Parkersville. All of her housebound patients inquired about Ty and the trial. She told them what she could. That afternoon her office was nearly empty. It amused Amanda when she realized that the entire town was in the courthouse hearing the closing arguments and waiting for the jury's verdict. Amazing how they had all gotten well overnight.

"Inez?" She called her nurse. What the heck. There wasn't anything to do. "Want to go to Effingham?"

Inez must have been waiting for Amanda to ask. She popped her head around the corner. "Do birds fly?"

Amanda laughed. "Let's go, then."

It took at least an hour for Amanda to drive to the courthouse in the neighboring town. They parked and started up the steps just as a bunch of reporters started down. Amanda knew without asking that the jury verdict was in, and from the excitement she knew what it was, too. Ty and the Whittikers were standing in the doorway, smiling and shaking hands. Every reporter that hadn't run outside had gathered around the principals.

When Ty looked through the crowd he saw Amanda, smiled, and motioned her forward.

She had started toward Ty and was almost there,

when the prosecutor intervened. "Quite a testimony," he said.

"Thanks," Amanda answered.

"You were great, but I think Ty would have won even without you."

"Oh? Why's that?"

"He's brilliant."

Amanda smiled. "I think he's pretty special myself."

"You heard about his appointment, didn't you?"

"Excuse me?" Amanda's heart started to thud in trepidation. "What appointment?"

"He's been offered a political appointment," the prosecutor repeated. "Glenn Whittiker was taking care of it. It was contingent on winning the case, of course, but I'm beginning to think that was a foregone conclusion."

Amanda had a hard time standing there with a smile on her face. Her hands had started to tremble and she felt her chest tighten so that she could hardly breathe. *No*, her mind screamed. *Please don't let it be true*. Ty hadn't used her again. He wouldn't. Not after all they had shared.

"I'm pretty sure he's taking it. Actually, he'd be a fool to refuse. See you later," the prosecuting attorney went on, snapping his briefcase, "I guess I'll read about everything in the papers."

"I guess," Amanda managed to say.

"Be sure and give him my congratulations."

"I will."

She'd give it along with hers—only she had more than congratulations to give him. Ty was so busy, he didn't even realize she wasn't around. She shouldered her way to him. When he saw her, his eyes lit up with pleasure again. "Amanda."

She didn't bother with amenities. "Ty, did you know you were getting a political appointment out of this?"

Immediately his expression changed and he tried to take her hand. "Amanda, wait—"

"Did you know?" she insisted, pulling away. "Did you know about that political appointment?"

"Yes," he said at last, "I knew."

It all added up. He'd taken her out there to see Tommy. He'd made her feel sorry for the boy. "Damn you, Tyler Marshall." She wouldn't cry. She wouldn't give him the satisfaction of seeing her break down. "You probably knew about the epilepsy, too, and the drugs. You research so thoroughly. That's how you win trials, isn't it?"

"I'm supposed to win trials, Amanda."

"Oh, God, Ty, don't you have any principles at all?"

"Amanda, wait," he said, when she turned away, "let me explain."

She felt like she was back in Chicago all over again. Even then, the prosecuting attorney had been the one to break the news to her. She whirled around. "Explain what? Explain how you used me? How you manipulated me? And this whole trial? How you got more fame and notoriety? How you got a political appointment?" The last she nearly spat out. "No, thanks. You can spare me the details."

With that she turned and walked quickly away.

Ty tried to follow her, but there were so many reporters blocking his way he couldn't get through the crowd. "Amanda!" he called one last time. "Dammit, Amanda, wait for me."

She just kept walking.

Amanda refused to answer her door or her phone. Ty came by about an hour later, but she pretended she wasn't home. He finally left, giving up. Then he called. Then he came back. He stood with Mrs. Crowley on the lawn and shouted to her. "Amanda, I love you!"

She ignored him, just like she was going to ignore the hurt that tore at her insides. But she couldn't ignore the tears streaming down her face.

"Amanda, answer me," he called again. "Look, I'm sorry. Please, let me explain."

She sat stoically at her kitchen table, refusing to look outside, trying not to listen.

"Mandy Lou?" Mrs. Crowley knocked. "I'm feeling a mite peaked, dear. I wondered if I could see you for a minute?"

"I'm taking the day off," Amanda answered, still not opening the door. "If you're really sick, go to the hospital in Parkersville."

She could hear the woman talking to Ty. Then they both went away. But Ty came back not more than five minutes later. "Amanda, if you don't let me in, I'm going to break down the door."

"I'll call Sheriff Toombs," she answered.

"Mandy, I love you."

She shook her head. How could he love her and have betrayed her this way? "I don't want to see you, Ty. Please go away."

"How about tomorrow? Will you see me then?"

"No."

"Dammit, Amanda, I didn't take the political appointment. I never intended to in the first place. I knew about it, but I came here for you."

"Don't lie to me, Ty."

"If you'd see me, I could explain everything."

"I don't want your explanations."

He sighed. A few minutes later she heard someone else talking to him and then silence.

Ty didn't come back the rest of the evening, but then Amanda hadn't expected him to. In fact, she didn't expect ever to see him again. He'd made his choice a long time ago, two years ago to be exact, and it hadn't been her.

Chapter Ten

AMANDA CRIED MOST OF the night. The next morning she sounded as if she were speaking through a foghorn, and her eyes were red and swollen. As usual she had office hours, but today, since it was Friday, she was seeing patients early and going to the hospital late. The only thing she could do was pretend nothing had happened.

Inez was already in the office when Amanda came through with her morning cup of coffee. The place was packed. She glanced around at all the people, who were difficult to ignore. "What are they doing here? What does everyone want?"

"I guess they're sick," Inez answered.

"Miss Gertrude hasn't been here in three weeks," Amanda said. Mrs. Crowley was sitting there, too, along with Mr. Crowley, and even Miss Mabel had made it in to the office.

"Then I guess it's time she was checked. By the way," Inez continued, "in case you're wondering, I have an opinion now."

Amanda glanced at her nurse. "About what?"

"Tyler Marshall."

She turned away. "I'm not wondering."

"Just for the record, Amanda," Inez said, "I think you're a fool."

Turning back, Amanda grabbed a chart from the nurse without comment. "Who's our first patient?"

"Tyler Marshall."

Amanda placed the chart down.

"You can't refuse to see him," Inez went on saying. "He's sick."

"Sure." She glared at her nurse and then glanced down at the medical history form she asked all new patients to fill in. To say that Ty had taken a few liberties would be an understatement. If she wasn't so irritated, she might have found his answers amusing. Along with his name and address, the house on Main Street, Ty had filled in other answers with tongue-in-cheek messages. Or at least she hoped they were tongue-in-cheek. Under "major complaint," he'd listed "sharp heart pain, two years duration, only recently re-occurring, and lasting all night long." For "sex," he'd filled in "There's only one woman in my life. That's all there will ever be."

"I wonder who that is?" Inez remarked, following Amanda's gaze.

"I wonder," Amanda answered. "Who set this up?"

"What do you mean?"

"Don't play dumb with me, Inez. You're not as

folksy as everyone else in this town. What's Ty doing here?"

"He wants to talk to you."

"Fine. The man wants to talk, I'll talk." Furious, Amanda headed for the examination room. She was tired of his antics, but if Ty wanted to play games, she could play them, too.

Ty was sitting on the examination table, undressed with only a sheet covering the lower half of his body. "Good morning, Mr. Marshall," she said as she walked into the room and headed to the sink to wash her hands. She had decided to act serious, but it was difficult to ignore his broad chest and tanned physique. "I see you're not feeling well. What's the problem today?"

"I'm sick," he answered.

"What kind of sick?" She glanced down at the chart as she dried her hands.

"I hurt."

"Where?"

"My chest."

"I see." Inez had taken his vital signs. Amanda pulled out her stethoscope from her pocket. "Well, why don't you lie down and we'll have a look."

"Are you angry at me, Amanda?"

"Why would I be angry at you?"

"About yesterday."

"I have no idea what you're talking about. Does yesterday have anything to do with your illness?"

"Yes, it's what's caused all my pain."

"Then there's no reason for me to be angry with you." Playing the game, Amanda listened to his heart, which sounded so healthy it was disgusting, and then to his breathing. She wished she was in as good shape.

She touched his chest. "Is this where it hurts?"

"No, lower. My stomach."

"I thought you had chest pains."

"I did, but my stomach hurts now."

Trying to remain detached, she tucked the sheet lower and slid her hand down his muscled abdomen, touching him every so often, gently probing. The dark hairs prickled her palms and she felt his eyes on her, searching.

"There?" she asked.

"No," he said huskily, "just a little lower."

She glanced at him, thinking he would look away, but he met her gaze. His expression was serious.

"Remember how it was between us, Mandy?" he murmured, stroking his hand up her arm. "I do."

"Don't, Ty."

"Remember the nights?"

That was the last thing she wanted to remember. The times they had made love. She jerked away. "What are you trying to prove?"

"Nothing. Can't you give me a chance, Mandy?"

"No." She placed her stethoscope back in her pocket and turned to a cabinet. Ty watched her as she pulled out a syringe and a bottle of sterile water. She swiped the top of the bottle across an alcohol-laden cotton ball.

"What are you doing?"

She turned around, slipping the needle into the bottle as she did so. "I'm preparing a placebo," she said. "It's a make-believe treatment for a make-believe illness."

Ty sighed. "If you don't mind, I think I'll skip the shot," he said. "I don't think I'm that ill."

"Are you sure? I don't want you suffering when a shot would cure it."

He shook his head. "Amanda, I want to talk to you, not get a shot. I had no idea Tommy Whittiker had epilepsy. I had no idea you would discover a disease."

"You took me out there. You made me feel sorry for him. And for you."

"I took you out there because I wanted to be with you. I love you, Amanda, and if that isn't good enough, then I don't know what else to do."

"You knew about the political appointment."

"Yes, I knew. I told you that yesterday. I explained it to you, but you don't believe me, do you?"

"No."

"You know, Amanda, I'm really tired of defending myself to you." All of a sudden his expression changed and he started reaching for his clothes, shoving them on. "I've tried to explain. I've come here and made a fool of myself. I've done everything possible to convince you that I love you, but I've finally figured out that you don't want to believe me."

"You deceived me, Ty."

"I haven't deceived you. You want to think I've deceived you, I don't know why, but I don't care anymore."

"What about the appointment, Ty? Explain that."

"I already have, and even if I didn't, sometimes, in a relationship, you just have to have faith."

"Blind faith, like you had in Tommy?"

"The kid didn't do it, did he?" And with that last remark he walked out the door.

Amanda was as surprised to see him go as she had been to see him at all. She stood, watching him stride out the door. The best thing that had ever come into her life was leaving.

Inez must have felt just as frantic. She poked her head around the door. "He's going, you know. He's leaving."

Amanda couldn't do anything about it. "Who's the next patient?"

"Dammit, Dr. Pearson, aren't you going to do anything? The man you love is leaving."

What did Inez expect from her? Amanda walked into the waiting room. "How many of you are sick?"

Not a single person raised a hand.

She turned back to Inez. "Yes, I'm going to do something." She placed Ty's chart down. "I'm going to cry."

"What you ought to do is go after him," Jimmy John said, coming in the door. "He's leaving, Mandy Lou. He's leaving for good."

"He betrayed me," she said, though for the life of her she couldn't figure out why she was explaining it to the town mechanic. "Dammit, can't you understand that? He knew all about that political appointment."

"So what? He didn't take it. You know, once I had a mule that wasn't as stubborn as you, Mandy. I thought you might like to know that Bobby Martin finally told the newspapers Tommy didn't run him down on purpose."

"Why would I want to know that?"

"I heard tell you thought Tyler knew about the epilepsy."

"I did."

"Well, he didn't. Tommy told everybody this morning. Tommy told everybody that Tyler told him he was going to jail. Tyler told Tommy that for the first time, there was nothing he could do to help him. You owe Tyler an apology."

For a moment all Amanda could do was stand there and stare at the old man. "Oh, God."

"God is right. Tyler didn't know. If'n you hurry, you might be able to catch him. And maybe, just maybe he'll listen to you."

Amanda didn't wait any longer. She hurried out her door with everyone following and jumped into her car and drove to Ty's house as if all the demons of hell were chasing her. Thank goodness his Mercedes was still there. The other half of the town that hadn't been in her office this morning was also there. But she didn't care. She ran up the steps and pounded on the door. "Ty? Ty, are you there?"

He came to the door. "What do you want?"

"I'm sorry."

"So am I."

"Ty, please," she said, sensing his anger, his hurt. "I love you. Let me explain."

"Explain what?"

"I was being foolish. Stubborn and proud. I'm sorry I didn't believe you. You're right, sometimes you have to have faith."

"How does it feel, Amanda, to try to explain something and not get anywhere?"

"Not very good," she admitted. "Ty, please don't go."

He sighed. "I wish I could. They wouldn't let me."

She frowned. "What do you mean?"

He nodded to the crowd of people that had gathered closer, trying to listen. "They wouldn't let me leave. Actually, to be honest, I wouldn't have gone anyway. At least not yet. I left you once without demanding you listen. I figured I'd try one more time." He opened the door and came out, carrying a huge wooden sign. On it he had scrawled, "I love you, Mandy Lou Pearson." "You're stubborn, Amanda, but I'm awfully determined myself. Once you told me I could tell it to the world and you wouldn't believe me," he explained. "I figured I'd give it one more try. I figured I'd tell it to the world."

"Oh, Ty, I love you."

"I love you, too." He propped the sign on his porch and took her in his arms. "We have to make another one, though."

"Why?"

"Advertising both our professions. And we have to figure out which house to live in, mine or yours."

"We could live in one and practice out of another," she suggested. "Are you asking me to marry you?"

"I don't know about you, but I'm tired of the gossip. I figure we'd better make it legal."

He kissed her. A cheer went up from the crowd. Jimmy John was prancing around, hardly able to contain himself. "Hot damn!" he said. "And hallelujah!"

Miss Gertrude stepped forward. "Tyler, are you and Mandy Lou going to get married?"

"Yes," Ty answered. "Why?"

"I just wondered if you wanted to rent the honeymoon suite. It goes for fifty dollars a night."

Ty grinned and glanced at Amanda. "What do you think? Want to stay at the Rialto Arms for our honeymoon?"

It served him right. "Miss Gertrude," she said, "you've got yourself a customer."

"Oh, no," he groaned, "I forgot she listens through doors."

Amanda laughed.

He sobered. "Oh, well, I guess that's all right. We have the rest of our lives."

"You're sure you want to stay in Rialto?" she asked, still worried about his practice. He was a wonderful attorney, and she didn't want to see him give up his profession for her.

"Amanda, I hear it's a lot of trouble to go all the way to Effingham for a lawyer."

"But will you keep busy? This is a small town."

"Are you kidding?" Ty laughed. "Look how busy twelve hundred people kept you."

"I think it was a conspiracy."

"I think you're right."

Right then Sheriff Toombs stepped from the crowd. Amanda hadn't even noticed him. "Well, you won, Tyler," he said, handing Ty a hundred dollar bill. "Here you go."

Amanda was shocked. "Did you bet on winning the case?"

"No," Ty said, "you bet on my winning the case. In fact, you'd better pay off. I bet on winning you, but I spotted him a week."

"Ty!" Amanda started to admonish him, but before she could say anything, he kissed her.

"Don't forget," he said, "it's all a matter of faith."

COMING NEXT MONTH

WINDOW ON TOMORROW #458
by Joan Hohl

Andrea Trask can't believe it: earth-studies professor Paul Hellka is the man of her dreams—literally! As ideal in reality as in fantasy, there's also something *very* mysterious about him...

SIMPLY MAGIC #459
by Carole Buck

One meeting with eccentric anthropologist Meade O'Malley has Brooke Livingstone intrigued. But it's going to take a lot to mend the shattered dreams of her past—and win her heart...

Order on opposite page